CW00543606

PRIVATE TUTORING

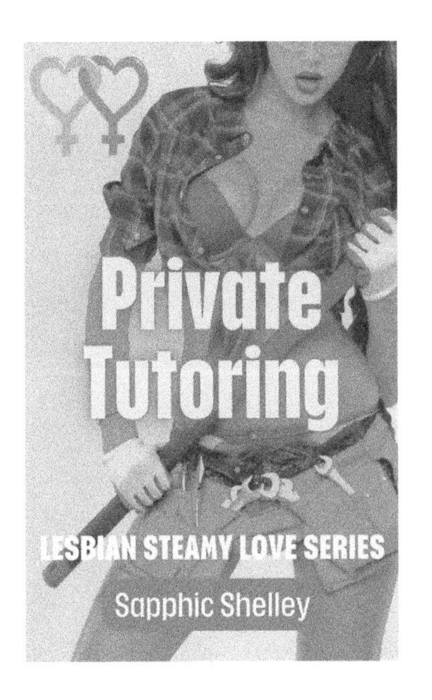

FOREWORD

Nineteen-year-old Jaqueline, a carpenter's apprentice, explores BDSM and develops her identity as a lesbian. She is determined to seduce her straight teacher and make her fantasies a reality despite obstacles.

CHAPTER ONE

Jackie's heart thudded loudly against her ribcage, echoing in her ears as she stood at the entrance of the BDSM club. The dimly lit corridor stretched out before her, a seemingly endless path that amplified her anticipation and nervousness. She took a deep breath, trying to steady herself and calm her racing thoughts. The heavy scent of sweat and arousal hung thick in the air, sending shivers down her spine.

"Here goes nothing," she whispered, steeling herself for what lay ahead. Her feet moved forward, each step feeling heavier than the last as she navigated through the darkness. Moans and gasps filled her ears, a symphony of pleasure and pain that only served to heighten her own desires.

As her eyes adjusted to the low lighting, Jackie

began to discern various scenes taking place around her. In one corner, a woman was bound in intricate rope work, suspended from the ceiling as her partner teased and pleased her. In another corner, a man was on his knees, obediently worshiping the heels of his female dominant. Everywhere she looked, there were displays of submission and dominance that left her both intrigued and slightly intimidated.

But as she made her way further into the club, Jackie felt a sense of liberation wash over her. This was where she belonged, among others who understood and embraced their deepest desires. And with newfound confidence, she continued on her journey through this world of pleasure and pain.

As Jackie stepped into the dimly lit room, she couldn't believe her eyes. The walls were lined with various instruments and tools, from whips and paddles to ropes and chains. In the center of the room, a group of people gathered, their bodies entwined in elaborate positions that Jackie had only ever read about in books or seen in movies. She could feel her heart racing as she took in the raw, unapologetic displays of desires and fantasies.

A tingling warmth spread between her legs as her body responded to the sights and sounds, causing her cheeks to flush with excitement. Just as she was taking it all in, a sultry voice murmured into her ear, sending shivers down her spine.

"Quite the sight, isn't it?" the voice said, its tone dripping with seduction.

Jackie turned her head to see who had spoken and found herself captivated by the woman standing beside her. Cassie Roberts was a vision of dominance, her jet black hair cascading down her back, framing the sharp angles of her face. Her slender figure was adorned in a tight, leather corset that accentuated every curve, while thigh-high boots encased her long legs. She exuded an aura of authority that demanded attention.

"Y-Yes," Jackie stammered, unable to tear her eyes away from Cassie's piercing gaze. "I've never seen anything like this before." The air around them seemed charged with electricity as they stood there, their eyes locked in a silent exchange.

Cassie's lips curled into a devious smirk as she drank in Jackie's awestruck expression with satisfaction. "Never been to a club like this before, have you?" she purred, her voice oozing with seductive confidence.

Jackie nodded, her heart pounding in her chest as she felt the weight of Cassie's gaze upon her. She could sense the raw power radiating from this woman, and it both thrilled and intimidated her – igniting a deep craving within to explore and understand this dark, alluring world.

"Would you like me to be your guide, show you the ropes and teach you a thing or two?" Cassie offered, her voice dripping with temptation.

Jackie hesitated for a moment, torn between fear and fascination. But as she looked into Cassie's eyes, she felt an irresistible pull towards the dominant woman, her longing and desire overpowering any lingering doubts.

"Yes," Jackie breathed out, barely audible above the pulsing music of the club. "I want that...more than anything."

Cassie's voice dripped with honeyed seduction as she extended her hand to Jackie, beckoning her further into the dark recesses of the club. Jackie's heart raced with nervous anticipation as she grasped onto the supple leather of Cassie's glove, feeling a jolt of electricity shoot through her body.

As they moved through the pulsating sea of bodies, Jackie's senses were overwhelmed by a kaleidoscope of sensations – the smell of sweat and incense, the sound of moans and groans intermingled with the beat of music, and the sight of bodies entwined in various states of undress.

"Trust, communication, and consent," Cassie purred

as they weaved through the maze, passing by scenes that both intrigued and terrified Jackie. She watched in awe as a woman was expertly bound in intricate rope work, her eyes filled with a mixture of pleasure and pain.

"Consent," Jackie echoed, her voice barely audible as she took in the provocative sights around her, realizing that this world was built on a foundation of power dynamics and exploration.

Cassie's grip on Jackie's hand tightened, her eyes burning with a fierce determination. "Without consent, none of this is possible," she declared, her voice low and commanding. "But with it, we can explore the delicate balance of power between dominant and submissive – a dance of trust and surrender."

A shiver ran down Jackie's spine as Cassie spoke, her heart racing with anticipation. "Teach me," she pleaded, her voice trembling with desire. "I want to know...everything."

Cassie studied Jackie's face carefully, searching for any trace of doubt or hesitation. When she found none, a glint of excitement sparked in her eyes. "You're sure?" she asked, her tone almost daring.

Without hesitation, Jackie nodded, steeling herself for what was to come. A wicked smile spread across Cassie's lips. "Then let us begin," she purred, "but be warned – once we start, there's no going back. You'll be pushed to your limits, facing pleasure and pain unlike anything you've ever known before."

"I'm ready," Jackie declared, her emerald eyes blazing with determination and desire. "Show me what this world has to offer."

Cassie's lips curled into a wicked grin as she led Jackie deeper into the club, her voice low and husky as she explained the principles and practices of BDSM. "We'll start with something simple, like restraint," she said, her words sending shivers down Jackie's spine. "But don't worry, we'll work our way up from there."

The mere thought of being restrained caused a rush of excitement to course through Jackie's veins. Her mind flooded with images of the bound woman she had seen earlier, fueling her eagerness even more.

"Restraint?" Jackie inquired, unable to mask the tremor in her voice.

"Indeed," Cassie replied with a sly smile. "But before we begin, we must establish some ground rules - for your safety and mine." She leaned in close, her breath hot against Jackie's ear. "We will use safe words, communicate constantly, and trust each other completely."

As they delved deeper into the realm of BDSM, Jackie's initial trepidation slowly began to dissipate, replaced by a burning curiosity and an insatiable hunger for knowledge. Under Cassie's expert tutelage, she learned about the various tools and techniques used in the lifestyle, as well as the psychological components that underpinned each interaction.

"Remember," Cassie reminded her, as they paused to observe a scene involving a flogger and a blindfolded submissive, "the true power in BDSM lies not in physical dominance, but in the ability to connect on a deep, emotional level with your partner. Trust, vulnerability, and understanding are the cornerstones of any successful BDSM relationship."

Jackie nodded, her thoughts racing as she considered the implications of Cassie's words. She felt herself drawn to this new world, captivated by the intensity and passion that seemed to permeate every inch of the club. And as she looked up at Cassie, her heart swelling with gratitude and admiration, Jackie knew that she had found a mentor who would guide her through the darkness and into the light.

The club was dimly lit, the scent of leather and sweat hanging heavy in the air. Jackie followed Cassie through a maze of rooms, each showcasing a different aspect of BDSM. Her heart raced with anticipation and desire as she prepared to dive headfirst into this new world.

Cassie's voice was low and alluring as she led Jackie towards a dark, secluded room. Inside, several couples were entwined in webs of ropes and chains, their bodies contorted into positions that seemed both agonizing and exhilarating. Cassie pointed to a woman suspended from the ceiling in intricate shibari rope work, her body exposed and vulnerable. "This is the art of bondage," Cassie whispered, her eyes glittering with excitement. "It's an intense form of connection between two people, but it requires skill and safety." As Jackie watched, a fire ignited within her, craving to experience this same level of passion and submission.

Cassie wasted no time in introducing Jackie to the world of impact play. With a glint in her eyes, she led Jackie through a range of instruments - from floggers and paddles to riding crops and canes.

“This is how we release our desires, our frustrations," Cassie explained with a devilish smile.

"It can be sensual, or it can be intense, but always remember to communicate with your partner and make sure they're enjoying every moment."

As Jackie watched a woman expertly wield a flogger, each strike against her partner's skin igniting a mix of pleasure and pain, she felt an unfamiliar heat burning within her.

Ripples of apprehension and arousal coursed

through her as she imagined herself in the submissive's place, eagerly anticipating the next sharp sting of leather against her flesh.

Cassie's voice dripped with authority as she led Jackie into a dimly lit room, the sound of heavy chains clinking filling the air. In the center of the room, a man knelt at the feet of his dominant partner, his body adorned only in a collar and leash.

"Power exchange is the cornerstone of BDSM relationships," Cassie explained, her gaze glinting with excitement. "One person surrenders control completely, while the other takes on the responsibility for their pleasure and well-being."

Jackie's cheeks flushed as she watched the submissive man eagerly obey every command from his dominant, their connection palpable and electrifying. "Is it always so intense?" she asked, unable to tear her eyes away.

"Intensity varies in every relationship," Cassie responded. "But for some, total surrender and obedience are essential elements. As long as both parties consent and find fulfillment in their roles, anything is possible."

As Jackie soaked in each new experience, she felt herself drawn deeper into the world of BDSM, captivated by the intensity and passion on display. Her body hummed with need, her mind racing with fantasies and desires she had never before allowed herself to acknowledge.

"Listen carefully, trust, communication and consent are absolute requirements in all BDSM interactions," Cassie's grip tightened on Jackie's shoulder as she spoke in a stern voice. "If you choose to delve deeper into this world, I will be your guide every step of the way."

Tears welled up in Jackie's eyes as she whispered her thanks. Every breath felt like fire in her lungs as they continued down the path, knowing that her journey would forever alter her existence. She couldn't contain her excitement for what lay ahead, eager to surrender herself to the unknown depths of pleasure and pain that awaited her.

CHAPTER TWO

In the dimly lit corner of the club, Jackie found herself chained to a St. Andrew's cross, her wrists and ankles secured by leather cuffs. The smell of sweat and arousal permeated the air as Cassie stood before her, wielding a flogger with expert precision. With each strike, Jackie's breath hitched, her body instinctively seeking to lean into the sensation.

"Focus on your breathing," Cassie instructed, her voice firm yet soothing. "Feel the leather against your skin, and let yourself be present in this moment."

Jackie closed her eyes, concentrating on the rhythm of her breaths, the heat radiating from her body, and the delicious sting of the flogger as it connected with her flesh. She felt both vulnerable and empowered, her trust in Cassie growing stronger with each passing second.

"Good girl," Cassie praised, pausing to run her fingers tenderly over Jackie's reddened skin. "You're doing so well."

"Thank you, Mistress," Jackie responded, her voice barely audible. The words felt foreign yet thrilling on her lips, solidifying the dynamic between them.

As their sessions continued, Jackie found herself eagerly anticipating each new lesson. Together, they explored sensation play, using ice cubes and hot wax to create a tantalizing contrast on her sensitive skin. They experimented with different types of restraints, from rope to handcuffs, and Jackie reveled in the feeling of surrendering control to Cassie.

"Always have a safeword," Cassie reminded her one evening, as she secured a ball gag around Jackie's head. "If at any point you feel uncomfortable or need to stop, just use your safeword and I'll immediately release you."

"Green," Jackie mumbled around the gag, the taste of silicone filling her mouth. It was a simple, yet vital reminder of the importance of trust and communication within their relationship.

"Perfect," Cassie replied, smiling warmly. "Remember, submission is a gift, and as your dominant, it's my responsibility to ensure your well-being at all times."

In between scenes, Jackie found herself opening up to Cassie about her past experiences, her fears, and her dreams. They shared intimate conversations late into the night, their connection deepening with each word spoken. Jackie yearned to please Cassie, not only in the playroom but in every aspect of their lives.

"Your willingness to learn is truly inspiring," Cassie told her one evening, as they shared a bottle of wine on the couch. "You've come so far in such a short amount of time, and I'm proud to be a part of your journey."

"Thank you for everything," Jackie said, her eyes glistening with unshed tears. "Without your guidance, I never would have discovered this side of myself. I want to keep exploring, to push my limits and become the best submissive I can be."

"Then that's exactly what we'll do," Cassie promised, raising her glass in a toast. "Together, we'll continue to explore the depths of your submission and unlock the full potential of our dynamic."

As Jackie clinked her glass against Cassie's, she knew that she was more than ready to embrace the challenges and rewards that lay ahead. Under Cassie's watchful eye, she would flourish, her true self finally set free.

~

THE DIMLY LIT room was filled with the scent of jasmine and the flickering glow of candles, casting shadows on the walls as Jackie lay on her back, her heart pounding in her chest. The silk restraints that bound her wrists to the bedposts felt both confining and liberating. Cassie stepped into her line of sight, a warm smile gracing her lips.

"Are you ready, my dear?" Cassie asked softly, her fingers tracing the soft curve of Jackie's thigh.

"Y-yes," Jackie stammered, feeling both excitement and trepidation course through her veins. She bit her lip, struggling to find the words for what she wanted to share. "Cassie, there's something I need to tell you."

"Of course, sweetheart. You can tell me anything," Cassie reassured her, her touch gentle and comforting.

Jackie took a deep breath, gathering her courage. "I've been feeling something...unexpected. I think I'm attracted to my teacher, Marissa."

Cassie didn't flinch or show any signs of judgment; instead, her gaze remained steady and understanding. "It's natural to develop feelings for someone who has a significant impact on our lives. But remember, it's important to recognize when these feelings are appropriate and when they are not."

"I know," Jackie whispered, her eyes shimmering with vulnerability. "Marissa is married and identifies as straight. I also know the boundaries between student and teacher should be respected. It's just...hard."

"Attractions can be complex," Cassie agreed, brushing a lock of hair away from Jackie's face. "But part of the journey we're on together is learning how to navigate these complexities in a healthy way."

As Cassie spoke, Jackie felt a renewed sense of trust and gratitude wash over her. Cassie had always been there to support her, guiding her through the delicate intricacies of the BDSM lifestyle and helping her understand her own desires.

"Thank you, Cassie," Jackie murmured, her voice thick with emotion. "Your support means everything to me."

"Always," Cassie replied, pressing a tender kiss to Jackie's forehead. "Now, let's focus on tonight. Remember, aftercare is a crucial part of our play. I'll be here for you, every step of the way."

As Cassie began to expertly caress Jackie's body, the young woman allowed herself to sink into the sensations, her mind gradually releasing the worry and confusion that had plagued her thoughts. She surrendered herself completely to Cassie's skilled touch, knowing that the emotional and psychological aspects of their relationship would be nurtured and protected.

"Trust me, Jackie," Cassie whispered, her breath

warm against Jackie's ear. "Together, we'll explore the depths of your desires, and I'll always be here to catch you when you fall."

With those words, Jackie felt a surge of warmth envelop her, her heart swelling with love and appreciation for the incredible woman who had opened up a world of possibilities for her. Radiating gratitude and desire, she nodded, signaling her readiness to continue their journey together.

THE FLICKERING CANDLELIGHT cast a warm glow over Jackie's trembling body as she lay on the soft sheets, her wrists bound delicately above her head. The blindfold she wore heightened her senses, making every touch electrifying.

"Are you ready, Jackie?" Cassie's voice was smooth and sultry, a reassuring presence in the darkness.

Jackie swallowed her nerves, her heart pounding in her chest. She could feel herself growing more confident, embracing her desires and fantasies under Cassie's guidance. "Yes," she whispered, her voice steady and determined.

"Good girl," Cassie praised, running her fingertips

gently down Jackie's exposed torso. The sensation sent shivers down her spine, igniting a fire within her. "Now, I'm going to introduce you to something new. Remember, if it becomes too much, just use your safeword."

"Understood," Jackie replied, anticipation coursing through her veins.

She felt Cassie straddle her hips, the warmth of her mentor's body radiating against her own. Then, the first droplet of hot wax landed on Jackie's abdomen, causing her to gasp sharply. It was an intense, searing heat that quickly dissipated into a dull throb.

"Is it too much?" Cassie asked in a concerned tone.

"No," Jackie breathed, surprising herself with her eagerness for more. She had come so far since entering this world of BDSM, and she wanted to explore further.

"Good," Cassie murmured, continuing to drizzle the hot wax in intricate patterns across Jackie's sensitive skin. With each droplet, Jackie felt herself submitting deeper to the sensation, trusting in Cassie's expertise and care. She marveled at how far she'd come under her teacher's guidance.

"Remember to breathe, love," Cassie reminded her gently. Jackie took a deep breath, focusing on the rhythmic rise and fall of her chest as it mingled with the heat encasing her body.

"Thank you, Cassie," Jackie whispered, her voice laced with gratitude and desire. "I trust you completely."

"Trust is everything," Cassie replied, trailing her fingers through the cooling wax. The sensation was indescribable, a perfect blend of pleasure and pain that sent shudders rippling through Jackie's body.

As the session continued, Jackie felt herself growing bolder, more willing to explore the depths of her desires. She had come to understand the importance of communication and consent in the BDSM lifestyle, and with Cassie by her side, she knew she could safely push her boundaries.

When the time came for their scene to end, Cassie gently removed the blindfold and untied Jackie's wrists. As they lay entwined on the bed, their breathing gradually returning to normal, Jackie couldn't help but feel a newfound appreciation for the BDSM lifestyle. It was a world where she could fully embrace her desires and fantasies, guided by an incredible woman who understood her implicitly.

"Thank you, Cassie," Jackie murmured, pressing a tender kiss to her mentor's lips. "I can't wait to see what else you have to teach me."

"Neither can I," Cassie replied, her eyes sparkling

with pride and affection. "Together, we'll explore every aspect of this beautiful lifestyle."

And as they drifted off to sleep, wrapped securely in each other's arms, Jackie knew that there was so much more to discover, and she couldn't wait to continue her journey under Cassie's guidance.

CHAPTER THREE

Jackie's heart pounded in her chest as she approached the unassuming entrance to the BDSM club again. The flickering neon sign above the door cast an eerie glow across her determined face, accentuating the sharp angles of her cheekbones and the intensity in her bright green eyes. Steeling herself, she took a deep breath and pushed open the door.

Inside, the atmosphere was electric. Dimmed lights, deep red walls, and the sound of clinking chains filled the air, sending chills down Jackie's spine. Her pulse quickened as she scanned the room for Cassie, her gaze finally coming to rest on her striking mentor.

"Jackie," Cassie called out, her jet-black hair cascading gracefully over her slender shoulders. She closed the distance between them, her heels clicking authoritatively against the floor. "I'm glad you could make it back."

"Hi, Cassie," Jackie replied, trying to keep her voice steady despite the pounding in her ears. "I'm excited to return."

Cassie offered a reassuring smile, her dark eyes searching Jackie's face. "Before we start again, it's important that we reestablish trust and communication in our relationship. In the world of BDSM, these are the pillars that hold everything together."

"Trust and communication," Jackie echoed, nodding slowly as she mentally prepared herself for this new experience. Her fingers nervously toyed with the hem of her shirt, betraying her inner turmoil.

"Exactly," Cassie continued. "As we explore this lifestyle together, I need you to know that I will always have your best interests at heart. Your safety, consent, and well-being are my top priorities. Likewise, you should always feel comfortable discussing your thoughts and feelings with me."

Jackie felt warmth radiating from Cassie's words, easing some of the tension in her body. "I understand, and I promise to be open with you," she said, her voice growing stronger.

"Good," Cassie replied, a hint of a smile playing at

the corners of her lips. "Now, are you ready to begin your second training session?"

A sudden surge of excitement coursed through Jackie's veins, pushing away the last of her trepidation. She straightened her posture, her green eyes meeting Cassie's dark gaze with newfound confidence. "Yes, I'm ready."

"Let's get started then." Cassie extended her hand, inviting Jackie to follow her deeper into the world of BDSM. As Jackie took it, she couldn't help but marvel at the thrilling adventure that lay ahead, knowing that with Cassie as her guide, she would navigate this new landscape with both skill and passion.

CASSIE LED JACKIE into a dimly lit room, the air thick with anticipation. The walls were adorned with various implements of bondage – cuffs, chains, and ropes of all sizes and textures. As Jackie's eyes traced the intricate patterns of rope suspensions hanging from the ceiling, she felt her heart race, desire and curiosity intertwining within her.

"Welcome back to the world of bondage," Cassie said, her voice sultry yet firm. "Bondage can be an incredibly intimate and erotic experience, allowing you and your partner to explore vulnerability, trust, and surrender."

Jackie swallowed hard, her fingers twitching at her sides as she imagined the sensation of being bound, exposed and open to whatever Cassie had planned for her. She knew her carpentry skills might come in handy here, but she was eager to learn from her mentor.

"Where do we start?" Jackie asked, forcing her thoughts back to the present moment.

"Rope is one of the most versatile tools for bondage," Cassie explained, grabbing a soft, silken rope from the wall. "It allows for endless creativity when it comes to tying knots and creating patterns on the body."

As Cassie demonstrated a basic knot, Jackie marveled at the way her fingers moved deftly, weaving the rope into intricate loops and twists. The smooth texture of the rope seemed like an extension of Cassie's body, and Jackie couldn't help but imagine how it would feel to be wrapped up in her embrace.

"Try this yourself," Cassie instructed, handing the rope to Jackie. "Start by finding the center of the rope, then wrap it around my wrist."

Jackie hesitated for a moment, her green eyes flickering with uncertainty. But as Cassie gave her a reassuring nod, Jackie's confidence swelled. She focused on the task at hand, finding the center of the rope and looping it around Cassie's slender wrist, following the pattern she had just demonstrated.

"Good," Cassie murmured, her dark eyes locked on Jackie's. "Now, make sure it's snug but not too tight. You want to restrain me without causing discomfort or cutting off circulation."

Jackie nodded, adjusting the tension of the rope as she continued to wrap it around Cassie's wrist. She felt a thrill of power at having her mentor in such a vulnerable position, but also a sense of responsibility, knowing that Cassie's safety was in her hands.

"Perfect," Cassie praised as Jackie completed the knot. "Next, I'll show you how to tie a chest harness, which can be both decorative and functional for restraint."

As Jackie watched Cassie demonstrate the more complex technique, she marveled at the way the rope seemed to dance between her fingers. The pattern formed a beautiful web across Cassie's chest, accentuating her curves and adding an artistic element to their play.

"Your turn," Cassie said with a seductive smile, handing Jackie a fresh length of rope.

As Jackie began to weave the harness around Cassie's body, she found herself getting lost in the rhythm of the knots and loops. Her fingertips brushed against Cassie's bare skin, sending shivers down her spine. The room faded away, leaving only the two of them, bound together by trust and desire.

"Beautifully done," Cassie whispered, her breath warm against Jackie's ear as she inspected the finished harness. "You have a natural talent for this, my dear."

Jackie flushed with pride, her heart swelling with gratitude for her mentor's guidance and encouragement. As they stood there, bound together by more than just ropes, Jackie knew she was ready to explore even deeper into this world of pleasure and surrender.

CHAPTER
FOUR

The dim, sultry atmosphere of the club pulsed with the sensual beat of music, every throb resonating within Jackie's chest. With the ropes now set aside, Cassie leaned in close, her lips brushing against Jackie's ear as she whispered, "Now that you've mastered the art of bondage, it's time to explore discipline."

"Discipline?" Jackie questioned, her breath hitching with anticipation.

"Exactly," Cassie replied, her eyes sparkling with mischief. "In BDSM, discipline can be an essential component of the power dynamic between dominant and submissive partners. It can take many forms, such as impact play or role-playing scenarios."

Cassie guided Jackie to a wall adorned with various

tools and implements, each one designed to deliver a unique sensation. Jackie's fingers traced the handle of a leather flogger, the softness of the suede tails contrasting with the weighty grip.

"Go on, give it a try," Cassie encouraged, her voice laced with seductive authority. She positioned herself before Jackie, her back turned and arms stretched out, offering herself up for this lesson in pleasure and pain.

Jackie hesitated, gripping the flogger tightly. She had never wielded such power before, but Cassie's unwavering trust in her fueled her determination to learn. With a deep breath, Jackie swung the flogger, its tails connecting with Cassie's skin in a satisfying snap.

"Good," Cassie praised, a shiver of delight coursing through her body at the sting of the impact. "Now, try again, but with more force."

Emboldened by Cassie's guidance, Jackie delivered another strike, putting more strength behind her swing. The sound of leather meeting flesh echoed throughout the room, and Jackie found herself entranced by the beautiful marks blossoming across Cassie's back.

"Very nice, Jackie," Cassie cooed, her voice betraying a hint of arousal. "Now, let's move on to something else."

Jackie looked around at the wall of implements, her eyes drawn to a sleek wooden paddle. She picked it up, admiring its polished surface and the way it fit snugly in her hand.

"Excellent choice," Cassie noted with approval. "Paddles can deliver a more concentrated impact than floggers, making them ideal for discipline and control."

As Jackie experimented with various strikes, each one more confident than the last, she found herself growing more attuned to Cassie's reactions – the subtle shifts in her posture, the soft gasps escaping her lips. It was exhilarating, this dance between pleasure and pain, and Jackie reveled in her newfound abilities.

"Amazing, Jackie," Cassie murmured, her breath ragged as she turned to face her eager student. "You have a natural affinity for this, but remember that communication is key. Always pay attention to your partner's signals, and never hesitate to check in with them."

Jackie nodded, her mind racing with thoughts of all the possibilities that lay ahead in this world of discipline and desire. She felt a strange mix of vulnerability and power, both humbled and emboldened by the trust placed in her hands. As she gazed into Cassie's eyes, seeing the pride and passion reflected within, Jackie knew she had only just begun to scratch the surface of her own depths and desires.

JACKIE'S HEART raced as she watched Cassie lay out an assortment of items on a nearby table. The warm, dimly lit room seemed to close in around her, heightening her anticipation and desire for the lesson that was about to unfold.

"Consent and negotiation are the cornerstones of any BDSM relationship," Cassie began, her voice steady and authoritative. "You must establish clear boundaries and choose a safeword to ensure your partner's well-being, as well as your own."

Jackie couldn't help but feel a flush creeping up her cheeks as she listened, her body buzzing with excitement at the thought of what was to come. She focused intently on Cassie's words, determined to learn all she could from her experienced mentor.

"Your safeword can be anything you like," Cassie continued, "but it should be something easily remembered and not commonly used during a scene. When you use your safeword, everything stops immediately, no questions asked."

Jackie nodded, her thoughts racing. What word would be right for her? It needed to be something strong, something that held meaning for her. And then it came to her – "Willow." It was the name of her childhood treehouse, a place of refuge and solace. A perfect choice.

"Willow," Jackie stated confidently, making eye contact with Cassie, who smiled in approval.

"Very well. Now, let's put this into practice with a role-playing exercise," Cassie suggested, gesturing towards the table with various restraints and toys. She picked up a blindfold and handed it to Jackie. "Why don't you start by putting this on?"

As the soft fabric covered her eyes, Jackie surrendered to the darkness, feeling both vulnerable and exhilarated. She sensed Cassie's presence next to her, guiding her hands to the table and placing a flogger in her grasp.

"Remember, communication is key," Cassie whispered close to Jackie's ear, sending shivers down her spine. "Listen for cues and be prepared to stop if you hear your safeword."

The weight of the flogger felt reassuring in Jackie's hands as she experimented with it, listening carefully to Cassie's breathy moans and gasps. She could feel her own arousal building, but she knew the importance of maintaining control and focusing on their shared experience.

"Harder, Jackie," Cassie urged, her voice laced with desire.

Jackie complied, striking with more force, eliciting a sharp cry from Cassie. She hesitated, unsure if she had gone too far

"Willow," Cassie uttered softly, and Jackie immediately dropped the flogger, concern flooding her mind.

"Are you okay?" Jackie asked anxiously, reaching out in the darkness to find Cassie's hand.

"Perfect," Cassie reassured her, a smile evident in her voice. "You did exactly what you were supposed to do. You listened, you stopped, and you checked in with me. That's the essence of trust in BDSM – knowing that your partner will respect your boundaries and prioritize your safety."

As Jackie removed the blindfold, blinking against the sudden light, she found herself filled with gratitude and admiration for Cassie. This world of power exchange and exploration was thrilling, but it was also deeply rooted in trust and communication. With Cassie's guidance, Jackie knew she was well on her way to discovering her true desires and pushing the limits of her own pleasure.

As the room settled back into a comfortable silence, Jackie's eyes drifted to a large leather chair at the edge

of the dimly lit space. Cassie followed her gaze, a knowing smile playing on her lips.

"Ah, that brings us to our next topic," she said, crossing the room gracefully and perching on the armrest of the imposing piece of furniture. "Submission."

Jackie approached, curiosity piqued as she studied the intricate patterns carved into the dark wood frame. The plush cushions seemed to beckon her, inviting her to sink into their embrace.

"In BDSM relationships, there's often a power exchange between the dominant and submissive partner," Cassie explained, her tone measured and informative. "The submissive willingly gives control to the dominant, allowing them to make decisions, guide the play, and take responsibility for both partners' well-being."

Jackie's breath hitched slightly, intrigued by the idea of relinquishing control to someone she trusted. She ventured, "So, submission... it's about trust?"

"Absolutely," Cassie affirmed, her jet-black hair framing her face as she nodded. "Trust is the foundation of any healthy BDSM relationship. And in return for their submission, the dominant partner offers care, protection, and guidance."

"Guidance?" Jackie asked, her green eyes searching Cassie's for understanding.

"Exactly," Cassie replied. "As a dominant, it's my responsibility to help you explore your desires and grow as a submissive. That could mean introducing you to different forms of submission, like service-oriented submission or sexual submission."

"Service-oriented?" Jackie questioned, her fingers absently tracing the edge of the cushion.

"Service-oriented submission is when a submissive derives pleasure from performing tasks or services for their dominant partner," Cassie elaborated, watching as Jackie absorbed the information. "It can be anything from cooking dinner to cleaning the house, or even more personal tasks like dressing or grooming."

Jackie's thoughts raced. She had always taken pride in her independence and self-sufficiency, but the idea of offering herself in service to someone she cared for stirred a warmth deep within her. It was an unfamiliar sensation, one that both excited and unnerved her.

"Jackie," Cassie said softly, capturing her attention once more. "You don't have to decide right now what kind of submission appeals to you. This is just the beginning of your journey, and part of the fun is discovering what resonates with you."

"Thank you, Cassie," Jackie murmured, grateful for the understanding and patience her mentor offered.

"Of course," Cassie replied. "Now, let's talk about sexual submission. This can involve anything from following orders during sexual play to allowing your partner to control your pleasure."

As Cassie delved into various scenarios and possibilities, Jackie felt a growing heat between her thighs. The idea of submitting sexually ignited something primal within her, a hunger she had never before acknowledged.

"Would you like to try a little exercise?" Cassie asked, her voice low and seductive.

"Y-yes," Jackie stammered, her cheeks flushed with anticipation.

"Good," Cassie purred. "Kneel down in front of me."

Trembling slightly, Jackie obeyed, sinking to her knees on the plush carpet. Cassie's legs parted, revealing the black lace panties that hugged her slender hips and did little to disguise her arousal. Jackie's mouth watered at the sight, her own desire echoing in her chest.

"Your task is simple," Cassie instructed, her eyes locking onto Jackie's. "I want you to give me pleasure with your mouth, but only when I say so. Do you understand?"

Jackie nodded, her breath coming in shallow gasps as she awaited Cassie's command. The power dynamic between them crackled in the air, and Jackie found herself more than eager to submit.

"Good girl," Cassie whispered, and Jackie's heart swelled with pride at the praise, ready to embrace her newfound desires under Cassie's expert guidance.

CHAPTER FIVE

Cassie's fingers lightly traced the curve of Jackie's throat, her touch both electrifying and comforting. "Close your eyes," she instructed softly, her breath warm against Jackie's earlobe. "Let yourself feel everything."

Jackie obeyed, shutting out the world around her until there were only sensations—Cassie's fingertips dancing across her skin, the heat radiating from their bodies, the sound of their mingled breaths.

"Your submission is a gift," Cassie murmured, guiding Jackie's hands behind her back and securing them with a smooth silk scarf. "It's something to be cherished and respected." The fabric tightened around her wrists, immobilizing her but not causing any discomfort.

As Jackie stood there, bound and vulnerable, she felt strangely liberated. It was as if giving up control had granted her permission to explore her own desires without fear or guilt.

"Lean forward," Cassie ordered, her voice firm but gentle.

Jackie did as she was told, bending at the waist and presenting herself to her mentor. She heard the whisper of fabric as Cassie removed her panties, and the sudden sensation of cool air on her exposed flesh sent shivers down her spine.

"Remember," Cassie said, her tone a mix of soothing and stern, "you can call your safeword at any time. But I want you to try to push through your limits, just a little bit."

"Okay," Jackie whispered, her heart pounding in her chest.

The first crack of the flogger against her bare ass was a shock, making her gasp involuntarily. But it wasn't pain so much as surprise, as the sensation quickly dissolved into a warm, tingling pleasure that spread throughout her body.

"Good girl," Cassie praised, landing another strike that brought forth a moan from Jackie's lips. "You're doing so well."

As the rhythmic impacts continued, Jackie surrendered herself to the experience, allowing the sensations to wash over her like waves crashing upon a shore. Each strike pushed her closer to the edge of ecstasy, as her world narrowed down to Cassie's touch, her voice, and the sweet surrender of submission.

Finally, when Jackie could take no more, she breathlessly whispered her safeword. The flogging ceased immediately, replaced by Cassie's comforting embrace as she held Jackie close, murmuring words of reassurance and praise.

"Let's sit down and talk about what you just experienced," Cassie suggested after giving Jackie a moment to catch her breath.

As they sat on the couch, their bodies still flushed with arousal, Jackie tried to put her feelings into words. "It was...intense," she admitted. "But in a good way. I felt so connected to you, and to myself."

Cassie nodded, her eyes warm and understanding. "That's one of the beautiful things about BDSM: it can help us connect with our partners and ourselves on a deeper level. Do you have any questions or concerns?"

Jackie hesitated for a moment before asking, "What if I want to explore more? How do I know when I'm ready to push my limits?"

"Trust your instincts," Cassie advised, her hand resting reassuringly on Jackie's knee. "And always communicate openly with your partner. As long as you both feel safe and respected, there's no harm in exploring your desires."

Jackie took a deep breath, feeling both exhilarated and grounded by the experiences she had shared with her mentor. She knew that this was only the beginning of her journey into submission, but she felt well-equipped to navigate the uncharted waters ahead.

THE FAINT SCENT of leather and sweat still lingered in the air as Cassie's gaze met Jackie's, a knowing smile playing on her lips. The dim lighting cast a warm glow over the tangled ropes and cuffs that lay scattered around them, evidence of their recent exploration.

"Jackie, I'm really impressed with how open you've been to learning about BDSM and experiencing submission," Cassie began, her voice gentle yet firm. "But it's important for you to continue this journey on your own as well. I want you to do some research and explore different aspects of BDSM that interest you. Think of it as... homework."

Jackie's eyes widened at the mention of homework, but she quickly felt a spark of excitement ignite within her. The idea of delving deeper into this world thrilled her, and she was eager to learn more.

"Thank you, Cassie. I'll definitely do that," Jackie responded enthusiastically, already imagining the countless articles, videos, and stories she would immerse herself in. She couldn't help but feel a knot of anticipation forming in her stomach as she pictured the countless ways she could experiment and grow in her newfound passion.

"Good," Cassie replied, her voice full of approval. "Remember, knowledge is power – especially when it comes to understanding our desires and boundaries."

As they sat together, Jackie felt an overwhelming sense of gratitude for the woman who had opened her eyes to this new world. A world where she could explore the depths of her desires and truly connect with another person on a level she had never thought possible. She knew that without Cassie's guidance, she might have remained forever trapped in her uncertainty and confusion.

"Really, thank you, Cassie," Jackie said earnestly, her bright green eyes locking onto Cassie's dark ones. "Your mentorship has been invaluable to me, and I can't wait to see where this journey takes me."

Cassie's eyes softened, and she reached out to gently grasp Jackie's hand. "You're very welcome, Jackie. Just remember that this path is yours to walk. I'm here to guide you, but ultimately, your experiences and growth are up to you."

Jackie nodded, feeling a newfound sense of empowerment and determination surging through her veins. She knew that there would be challenges, insecurities, and fears along the way, but with Cassie by her side, she felt ready to face them head-on.

"Let's make a plan to meet again soon," Cassie suggested. "We can discuss your homework and any new questions or discoveries you've made."

"Absolutely," Jackie agreed, already looking forward to their next encounter. As they exchanged goodbyes and Jackie prepared to leave the club, she couldn't help but feel a rush of excitement at the thought of all the untapped potential waiting for her in this world of BDSM. And as she stepped out into the crisp night air, she felt more alive than ever before.

THE COLD METAL of the door handle sent a shiver down Jackie's spine as she stepped out of the club, leaving behind the intoxicating scent of leather and sweat that had filled her nostrils throughout her time with Cassie. The air outside was crisp and fresh against her flushed cheeks, a stark contrast to the heated atmosphere she had just emerged from.

"Goodnight, Jackie," called Cassie from the doorway, her voice warm and reassuring.

"Goodnight, Cassie," Jackie replied, her breath forming a visible mist in front of her face as she turned to walk away. Her heart pounded in her chest, the echoes of her newfound experiences lingering within her like an unquenchable fire.

As she walked down the dimly lit street, Jackie couldn't help but replay the events of the evening in her mind. The sensation of the ropes winding around her wrists, the sharp sting of the leather flogger against her backside, and the exhilarating feeling of vulnerability and power she experienced as she submitted herself to Cassie's guidance.

"God, I never knew it could be like this," Jackie whispered to herself, the sound barely audible above the crunch of her boots on the frosty pavement. She could still feel the phantom caress of the ropes on her skin, eliciting a shiver of anticipation for what might come next in her journey.

As the night progressed, Jackie found herself paying closer attention to the sensations that surrounded her – the cool breeze teasing her neck, the rough texture of the brick walls she brushed past, even the smoothness of her own fingertips as they traced idle patterns on her thigh. It was as if her senses had been heightened, amplified by her recent exploration into the world of BDSM.

"Is this what Cassie meant when she said that submission can bring a new level of awareness?" Jackie wondered aloud, her thoughts racing as she considered the implications of her newfound interests. The idea of being so attuned to her body and environment was both thrilling and daunting, but she knew that with Cassie's guidance, she could navigate this uncharted territory.

Jackie stopped for a moment, leaning against the cold brick wall of a nearby building as she let her thoughts wander. She imagined herself bound and helpless under Cassie's watchful gaze, her body trembling with anticipation as she awaited the next searing touch or whispered command. The images sent a wave of desire crashing through her, her breath catching in her throat as she felt her arousal surge.

"Fuck," Jackie muttered under her breath, her eyes darting around to ensure no one was in sight. Her hand slipped between her legs, the dampness there a testament to the overwhelming effect of her memories and fantasies. She bit her lip, fighting back a moan as she allowed herself a few stolen moments of pleasure before hastily pulling away.

"Alright, enough of that," she chastised herself, her cheeks burning as she resumed her walk home. The excitement of her newfound desires still buzzed within her, and she knew that resistance would be futile – but for now, she would have to content herself with the promise of future lessons and experiences.

As Jackie continued her journey home, one thing became abundantly clear: her life had been irrevocably changed by her encounter with Cassie and the world of BDSM. And though uncertainty and challenges undoubtedly lay ahead, she couldn't help but feel empowered by the knowledge and experiences she had gained, eager to explore the depths of her desires and see just how far they would take her.

CHAPTER SIX

The dimly lit room hummed with an electric energy, as shadows danced along the walls and the faint glow of candles flickered across the various BDSM equipment and props scattered throughout. A rhythmic, pulsating beat filled the air, blending with the sound of leather and metal, creating an intoxicating, seductive atmosphere.

Jackie stood in a secluded corner, her palms sweaty and heart racing with anticipation for the upcoming public demonstration. The dull thud of a flogger meeting flesh echoed through the club, sending shivers down her spine. Her bright green eyes scanned the scene, both excited and anxious about what lay ahead.

"Hey, are you ready? It's almost your turn," said a

sultry voice from behind her, startling Jackie out of her thoughts.

"Uh, yeah, I think so." Jackie stammered, rubbing her hands on her jeans to try to dry them off.

"Good, you'll do great. We're all here to support each other," the woman reassured her, placing a surprisingly warm hand on Jackie's shoulder.

As she turned to face the woman, Jackie felt the familiar conflict within her and intensify excitement at exploring this new world of dominance and submission, and anxiety about her own desires and her growing attraction to her teacher. She briefly closed her eyes, trying to center herself and focus on the task at hand.

"Thanks, that means a lot," Jackie managed to say, offering a small but genuine smile.

"Remember, just be yourself and enjoy the experience," the woman advised, giving Jackie's shoulder a reassuring squeeze before disappearing back into the crowd.

Taking a deep breath, Jackie mentally prepared herself for the moment she'd step onto the stage, her heart pounding against her chest like a hammer. This was her time to shine, her moment to share her newfound skills with the world. And even amidst the whirlwind of emotions coursing through her, she knew one thing for certain - she was ready to face whatever came her way.

WITH HER HEART pounding in her chest, Jackie stepped further into the dimly lit club. The low thump of electronic music filled her ears, creating a pulsing rhythm that seemed to echo the thrumming of her own pulse. She scanned the room, taking in the various BDSM equipment and props scattered throughout. Leather cuffs and chains, ropes coiled like sleeping snakes, and gleaming metal implements were all artfully arranged, each one a tantalizing promise of forbidden pleasures.

As Jackie observed the other participants, her nervousness was momentarily eclipsed by curiosity. Her eyes were drawn to a woman bound in intricate rope work, her body suspended above the ground as if floating on invisible waves. Another corner showcased a couple engaging in impact play, the sharp crack of a paddle against flesh punctuating the heavy bassline of the music. Elsewhere, she saw a domme expertly teasing her blindfolded submissive with an array of sensory toys, the sub's moans lost in the cacophony of sounds.

"Jackie, you're up next," a voice called out, jolting

her from her voyeuristic reverie. Her stomach tightened with anticipation, her palms suddenly slick with sweat. She had never performed in public before, and the thought of baring herself – both physically and emotionally – before this sea of strangers was almost overwhelming.

"Deep breaths, Jackie," she whispered to herself, attempting to center her thoughts and dispel the tendrils of anxiety threatening to engulf her. "You can do this."

Stepping onto the stage, Jackie hesitated for a moment, feeling the weight of the audience's gaze upon her. It was a mixture of curiosity, expectation, and something else she couldn't quite put her finger on - perhaps a touch of lustful intrigue. But then, as if sensing her uncertainty, the crowd began to cheer her on, their collective voices blending into a supportive roar that washed over her like a wave.

"Go on, Jackie! Show us what you've got!" someone shouted from the depths of the darkened room, their words puncturing the haze of fear and doubt that had settled over her.

Emboldened by their encouragement, Jackie took a deep breath and began her performance. Each movement was precise and deliberate, revealing the hours of practice she had devoted to honing her skills. As she navigated the delicate dance between power and surrender, she felt a surge of confidence and pride coursing through her veins, her previous anxiety melting away under the heat of the audience's rapt attention.

"Ready to do this?" Jackie murmured to herself, taking a deep breath as she glanced down at the flogger in her hand. The soft leather tendrils draped over her fingers like warm silk, their ends whispering over the stage with each subtle motion.

"Let's begin," she announced confidently, her voice carrying across the room and commanding the attention of the audience.

Her volunteer – a petite woman with fiery red hair and a sultry smile – stood before her, anticipation shining in her eyes. Jackie met her gaze, the unspoken understanding between them igniting a spark of excitement that surged through her veins.

"Are you ready?" Jackie asked her, receiving a nod and a barely audible "Yes" in return.

With practiced precision, Jackie began the dance of the flogger, her wrist flicking expertly to send the tendrils slicing through the air. Each impact against the woman's pale skin was accompanied by an intoxicating sound – a sharp crack followed by a low, resonant thud. The scent of leather filled the air, mingling with the faint aroma of sweat and arousal that perfumed the room.

"God, it feels amazing," the redhead purred, arching her back to offer more of her body to Jackie's skilled touch. "Don't stop."

"Trust me," Jackie replied with a wicked grin, her heart pounding in rhythm with each swing of the flogger. "I'm just getting started."

As the scene continued, Jackie found herself lost in the rhythm and sensation of it all - the weight of the flogger in her hand, the satisfying sting of leather on flesh, and the moans and gasps that spilled from her partner's lips. She reveled in the power and control the moment afforded her, feeling more alive than she had in years.

"More," the redhead begged, her voice ragged with desire. "Please, I can take it."

"Alright," Jackie agreed, her mind racing with the thrill of pushing boundaries. As she increased both the intensity and pace of her strikes, the room seemed to fade away, leaving only the two of them locked in their passionate exchange.

"Jackie..." the woman whimpered, her eyes fluttering shut as a shudder of pleasure coursed through her body. "That's... incredible."

"Thank you," Jackie whispered, warmth flooding

her chest at the praise. She knew she had executed the scene flawlessly, a testament to her dedication and skill.

As her heartbeat gradually returned to normal, Jackie allowed herself a moment to bask in the afterglow of her performance. The sound of heavy breathing and the occasional sigh still lingered in the air, a testament to the impact she'd made on both her partner and the audience. It was a powerful reminder of her capabilities, and of the exhilarating world she'd chosen to embrace.

CHAPTER SEVEN

With each precise and calculated strike of her flogger, Jackie could feel the energy in the room shift. The once tense and expectant audience now let out a collective breath, their expressions a mixture of awe and admiration.

The sound of leather meeting flesh echoed through the space, accompanied by soft gasps and moans from Jackie's partner. As she landed the final stroke, Jackie could see the deep red marks decorating her partner's skin, evidence of the pleasure she had provided.

"Absolutely," another spectator agreed, their eyes wide and fixed on Jackie with an unbreakable gaze. It was as if they couldn't bear to look away, so entranced were they by her performance. "I've never seen anything quite like it," they added in a hushed tone of awe.

With each comment, each whisper of praise, Jackie felt her confidence skyrocket. She had done more than just showcase her skills; she had enraptured the entire room with her talent and charisma. Her heart raced with excitement and exhilaration as she basked in the undivided attention of her audience.

The thrill was intoxicating, and she found herself craving even more applause and adoration. As she stood in the spotlight, she felt like a true star shining brightly for all to see.

Jackie stood before the eager audience, her voice dripping with seductive authority. The sound of their collective affirmation stirred a fire within her, igniting a newfound sense of dominance and control.

"Excellent," she purred, flashing a wicked grin at her partner. "But we're just getting started."

With a swift movement, Jackie seized a length of rope and reveled in its smooth yet sturdy texture as she expertly bound her partner's wrists. Each knot tightened her grip on the situation, feeding her hunger for power and pushing her to explore uncharted territory.

"Please," her partner pleaded, anticipation palpable in every breath. "I want more from you, Jackie. Show me your full potential."

With a sly grin, Jackie twirls the ropes in her hands like a master puppeteer. Her movements are deliberate and precise as she binds her partner's limbs with effortless skill, relishing in the power she holds over them. As the ropes tighten, she can feel the rush of desire coursing through her veins, driving her deeper into this seductive world.

"Look at her go," an awed voice whispers in the crowd. "She's a natural."

"She's something else," another voice agrees, their eyes glued to Jackie's every move. "I've never seen anything like it."

Jackie basks in the attention and admiration of the audience, her confidence growing with each passing second. She knows she is being watched, but instead of feeling self-conscious, she feels empowered. And as the final knot falls perfectly into place, Jackie surveys her mesmerized audience with satisfaction, knowing that this is only the beginning of her journey towards total domination.

Jackie's heart thumped against her ribcage like a wild animal trying to escape. Her body trembled with anticipation as she continued her performance, the bound woman before her nothing more than a willing canvas for her dark desires.

The anxious energy that had plagued her earlier had transformed into a fiery excitement, fueled by the hungry stares of the audience and her newfound confidence.

"Are you ready for more?" Jackie purred, her voice dripping with seduction. A nod from her partner sent an electric jolt through her body, their shared passion burning brighter than ever.

As Jackie reached for a flogger, her fingers dancing over the soft leather strands, a sudden surge of doubt flooded her mind. She had practiced with it before, but never in front of such a large and judgmental crowd. Could she control the pain and pleasure with the same skill and grace in this intense setting?

"Is everything alright?" Her partner's concerned gaze made Jackie hesitate, her grip tightening around the handle of the flogger. "I... I'm not sure," she admitted, feeling a shard of vulnerability pierce through her newfound confidence.

"Take a deep breath," Her partner's soothing words calmed her nerves. "You've been amazing so far. Just focus on us, and let the rest fade away."

Inhaling deeply, Jackie pushed aside her doubts and regained control of her emotions. With renewed determination, she prepared to take their play to even greater heights, leaving all fears behind as she embraced the intensity of their shared passion and desire.

Gritting her teeth, Jackie blocked out the thumping bass and drunken chatter of the club. Flicking her eyes open, she let out a determined growl, fueled by her partner's unyielding belief in her skills.

With a swift motion, Jackie lifted the flogger and brought it down with force against her lover's skin. Each strike was a release, shattering any doubts that lingered within her mind and replacing them with the intoxicating symphony of leather meeting flesh and her partner's cries of pleasure.

"Fuck, yes!" Her partner screamed, rapture etched on their face. "You're fucking amazing!"

Jackie's hand trembled with anticipation as she gripped the flogger, her heart racing with a mix of fear and excitement. But as she began to wield it with growing confidence, a surge of pride and power over-took her, giving her an intoxicating sense of control.

The trust and connection between Jackie and her partner fueled their shared passion, allowing them to push past their inhibitions and delve deeper into the uncharted territory of their wildest desires. With each crack of the flogger, Jackie could feel her own boundaries being pushed and shattered, igniting a fire within her that burned hotter than ever before.

"Harder," her partner gasped, lost in a haze of pleasure and pain. And Jackie obliged, unleashing all of her pent-up desires on her willing partner as they journeyed together towards an ecstatic climax unlike any they had experienced before.

As the last notes of the song drifted into the background, Jackie's fingers tightened around the handle of her flogger. Her heart raced like a wild stallion, but she was exhilarated by the thrill of what was to come.

"Are you ready?" she asked her partner, who nodded eagerly, her cheeks flushed with anticipation.

"I'm more than ready," the woman purred, her eyes glimmering with excitement.

With a final deep breath to steady herself, Jackie unleashed a rapid-fire series of perfectly placed strikes, each one striking their target with precision. The crowd erupted in gasps and cheers as they watched Jackie command the stage with confidence and passion. What had started as a timid performance had transformed into a powerful display of dominance and skill.

"Oh, Jackie... yes!" her partner cried out in ecstasy as she reached her climax, trembling beneath Jackie's expert ministrations. The room was filled with the scent of leather and sweat and desire as Jackie brought her partner to new heights of pleasure.

The deafening sound of applause filled the room as Jackie stood tall, basking in the overwhelming adoration of the crowd. Her chest swelled with pride as she met her partner's gaze, their eyes locking in a triumphant and powerful moment.

"Thank you," her partner whispered, tears shimmering in her eyes.

"Thank you," Jackie echoed, her voice trembling with emotion. "For always believing in me."

As they walked off stage hand-in-hand, Jackie couldn't help but feel a rush of exhilaration coursing through her body. The doubts that once plagued her were now a distant memory; replaced by an unshakable sense of empowerment and confidence. This public display of talent not only proved her abilities but also allowed her to embrace her true self without hesitation or fear.

"Jackie, you absolutely owned that stage," a fellow club member exclaimed, practically jumping with excitement. "I can't wait to see what you'll conquer next."

Jackie's eyes blaze with determination as she nods in agreement. The taste of victory still lingers on her lips, fueling a newfound confidence that courses through her veins like fire. She eagerly anticipates what the world of BDSM has in store for her, hungering for the next step in her journey.

As THE SUN'S rays peeked through the soft, billowing curtains and bathed Jackie's bedroom in a warm, golden glow, her eyes slowly fluttered open. She stretched her lithe body languidly, feeling the pleasant ache that lingered from the previous night's events. Her limbs still hummed with the residual pleasure of her triumphant performance – the sharp crack of the whip, the salty tang of sweat on her skin, the sounds of ecstasy ringing in her ears.

Lying there, basking in the afterglow, Jackie couldn't help but smile to herself. Last night had been nothing short of incredible.

"Morning, beautiful," Talia's voice called out from across the room, breaking through Jackie's happy reverie. She turned her head to see her best friend sitting on the edge of her bed, a steaming cup of coffee in hand.

"Hey," Jackie replied, her voice low and husky from sleep. "How long have you been up?"

"Long enough to make us both some coffee," Talia grinned, extending the mug towards Jackie. "Thought you might need it after your big night."

"Thanks," Jackie said gratefully, taking a sip and relishing in the comforting warmth of the liquid as it spread through her veins. "I still can't believe I actually did it."

Talia's eyes shone with pride as she admitted, "Neither can I." She reached out to take Jackie's hand in hers and squeezed it gently. "But you were amazing, Jackie. And I know this is just the beginning for you."

Jackie stared into her coffee cup, her mind a flurry of thoughts and emotions. Last night had been a revelation, a thrilling confirmation of her own power and abilities. Yet, amidst the rush of excitement, there was a lingering feeling that she couldn't quite shake off. It took her a moment to identify it, but when she did, the realization hit her like a bolt of lightning.

"Marissa," Jackie murmured, her green eyes clouded with uncertainty.

"Marissa?" Talia echoed, raising an eyebrow in confusion. "What about her?"

"Last night, while I was on stage... I saw her in the crowd," Jackie confessed, her voice barely more than a whisper. "And I couldn't help but wonder... what she thought of me." Her words trailed off as she remembered the way Marissa's piercing blue eyes had followed her every move throughout the performance. A mix of nerves and anticipation flooded through Jackie at the thought of facing Marissa's opinion of her.

Talia's words cut through Jackie like a knife, the reminder of her forbidden feelings for her teacher slicing deep into her heart. She set her coffee cup down with a trembling hand, the liquid inside sloshing over the rim in her agitation. "I can't help it," she confessed, her voice barely above a whisper. "Every time I close my eyes, all I see is her."

"Then you need to confront her," Talia urged, her tone firm and unwavering. "Before this consumes you completely and ruins everything."

Jackie swallowed hard at the thought of facing Marissa, her mind racing with fear and longing. But she knew that Talia was right - she couldn't continue to deny these intense feelings any longer. With a deep breath, she made a resolution to finally speak her truth to the woman who had captured her heart and soul, no matter the consequences.

Jackie's voice trembled as she took a deep breath, trying to steady her nerves. "I'll talk to her," she said, her words laced with determination and fear.

Talia gave her friend's hand a tight squeeze, her smile masking the worry in her eyes. "Good," she replied, her tone edged with urgency. "But let's not waste any more time. Finish your coffee and get ready. Today is going to be intense."

As Jackie gulped down the last of her coffee and prepared for the day ahead, a surge of anticipation mixed with dread coursed through her veins. She knew that whatever happened during her conversation with Marissa would change everything – for better or for worse.

CRAFTING A FANTASY

FOREWORD

Nineteen-year-old Jaqueline is a skilled carpenter's apprentice who spends her days crafting beautiful pieces of furniture and dreaming of her MILF teacher. With every passing day, her attraction grows stronger, and she can't help but imagine what it would be like to experience an intimate encounter with her. However, there's one major problem: her teacher is straight.

Despite the odds against her, Jaqueline is determined to find a way to make her fantasies come true. She begins to explore the world of BDSM beginner.

CHAPTER
ONE

The air hung heavy with the rich, earthy smell of sawdust, carried by beams of sunlight that filtered through the large windows of Hartman & Co. Carpentry. The golden rays illuminated the workshop floor, casting long shadows across the worn wooden boards. This family business was tucked away in a tranquil corner of the town, where the symphony of power tools and rhythmic hammering could be heard throughout the day.

It was a place steeped in tradition and pride, where generations of skilled artisans had poured their hearts and souls into every piece of wood that passed through their hands. The walls were adorned with tools and finished projects, each one a testament to the dedication and passion that flowed through this bustling workshop.

In the center of the bustling workshop, amidst the clatter of tools and whirring of machines, stood the apprentice carpenter, Jaqueline "Jackie" Hartman. Despite her young age of 19, she exuded a confidence and skill that rivaled even the most experienced craftsmen. Her dark hair was cropped short, revealing the strong line of her jaw and emphasizing her bright green eyes that seemed to sparkle with determination.

As she worked on her latest project, her hands moved with a grace and precision that could only come from years of practice. She ran them over the smooth surface of the wood, feeling every bump and groove until it met her standards of perfection.

Jackie's passion for carpentry radiated from every pore; from the way she held herself with a confident stance, to the way her eyes narrowed in concentration as she worked. And when she finally stepped back to admire her progress, a satisfied smile graced her lips, knowing that she had once again created something beautiful with her own two hands.

Jackie's hands were greasy and she was focused on tightening a bolt when a familiar voice called out, interrupting her concentration. She looked up to see her brother Declan, who had taken over the family business, leaning against the doorframe of the workshop. The smell of sawdust clung to his beard as he gave her a sly smile. "You're looking good, sis," he said.

Jackie grinned back at him and wiped the sweat from her brow with a rag. "Thanks, Dec. Just trying to make sure this piece is perfect before Marissa comes by."

Declan nodded in understanding and pushed off the doorframe, walking over to examine Jackie's work. "She'll be impressed, no doubt."

Declan's smirk twisted into a condescending sneer as he looked down at Jackie. "Marissa again? Do you worship the ground she walks on?"

Jackie's face flushed with anger and embarrassment, her fists clenching at her sides. She couldn't deny the admiration she had for Marissa Thompson, her teacher and mentor in woodworking. Marissa was a true master of her craft, and Jackie longed to reach that level of skill.

"Stop it, Declan," she snapped, her voice trembling with emotion. "I admire her, okay? Is that so wrong?"

Declan's laughter filled the room as he patted Jackie's head like a child. "Relax, little sis. It was just a joke," he said, his tone dripping with sarcasm. "But seriously, you've got some talent. I'll give you that."

A small smile tugged at the corners of Jackie's

mouth as she tried to brush off his mocking words. Deep down, she knew her brother was proud of her, but sometimes his teasing hit too close to home.

As Jackie forced herself to focus on her work, she couldn't shake the all-consuming thoughts of Marissa. Every time the woman crossed her mind, her heart raced with an almost unbearable intensity. It wasn't just her incredible skills or commanding presence that drew Jackie in; it was the way her eyes would ignite with passion when talking about a complex joinery technique, or the gentle curve of her smile as she offered unwavering support and admiration.

Jackie's mind was a chaotic mess of conflicting desires. She desperately fought against the growing attraction she felt towards Marissa, knowing that it was not only inappropriate but also forbidden. The fact that Marissa was straight and married only added to the complexity, making Jackie feel guilty and ashamed for her feelings.

But as she focused on carving intricate patterns into the wood, Jackie's hands shook with pent-up desire and longing. Every stroke of the chisel was an outlet for the passion that threatened to consume her. She couldn't control her heart, but she could pour all of her intensity and dedication into her work, determined to impress both her mentor and her brother with her talent and devotion..

The rich, earthy scent of sawdust filled the air, mingling with the sweet fragrance of cherry wood. Jackie's skilled fingers glided over the smooth surface of the table she was meticulously crafting. The warm rays of sunlight streamed through the large windows of her workshop, casting a golden hue on the various tools and projects scattered throughout. Her bright emerald eyes darted between the detailed design sketched on a sheet of paper and the table itself, ensuring that every curve and line was flawless.

"Just one more precise cut here," she murmured under her breath, her hands confidently guiding the chisel into the wood with practiced precision. The workshop hummed with creative energy as Jackie poured her heart and soul into each piece she crafted.

Just as Jackie finished the final delicate groove on her sculpture, the workshop door swung open with a soft creak. In walked Marissa Thompson, her wavy blonde hair cascading over her slender shoulders in loose curls. She was dressed impeccably in a form-fitting blouse that hugged every curve and a pencil skirt that accentuated her toned legs. Jackie couldn't help but hold her breath at the sight of her teacher's elegant yet practical appearance, her heart fluttering in her chest with admiration.

Marissa's bright red heels clicked against the tile floor as she made her way over to Jackie, her deep blue eyes sparkling with genuine interest. Jackie's heart raced at the sight of her mentor, and she tried to steady her voice as she greeted Marissa. "I've been working on that table leg design you suggested," she said, gesturing towards her workbench.

"Let me take a look," Marissa said, leaning in closely as she examined the intricate carving on the wood. As she did, Jackie couldn't help but notice the sweet scent of jasmine radiating off of Marissa's skin. Her cheeks flushed with both excitement and nervousness.

"Your attention to detail is truly impressive," Marissa praised, tracing her fingers lightly over the design. "You have a real gift."

Jackie's breath hitched in her throat as Marissa's soft fingers grazed against her hand, sending a jolt of electricity through her body. She fought to keep her composure, desperately trying to ignore the overwhelming desire coursing through her veins.

"Do you want to see something?" Marissa's voice was low and seductive, her eyes shining with unbridled passion. "I think it'll give your work that final touch it needs."

Despite the burning desire within her, Jackie couldn't resist the opportunity to learn from her skilled mentor. Every fiber of her being screamed for Marissa's touch, but she forced herself to nod in agreement. Little did she know, this would only fuel the raging inferno of longing within her.

Marissa eagerly led Jackie to another workbench, her hands moving with such fluidity and grace as she demonstrated a technique that would elevate the table to a masterpiece. Jackie couldn't help but steal glances at Marissa, mesmerized by her skill and beauty. But with each passing second, Jackie's internal struggle intensified -she knew Marissa was off-limits.

Pushing aside her feelings, Jackie focused on absorbing every ounce of knowledge Marissa shared. She refused to let her forbidden desires get in the way of becoming a master carpenter.

Marissa's lips grazed Jackie's ear as she whispered commands in a husky, commanding tone. "Hold the tool just like this and angle it downward," she instructed, her hand gripping Jackie's with fervent urgency.

The heat of Marissa's body pressed against Jackie's, their hips pressing together as they worked in perfect synchrony. The intensity of their collaboration sent electric jolts through Jackie's body, stirring up a deep yearning within her.

"Look at the intricate pattern it reveals," Marissa breathed, her voice dripping with seductive allure. Her finger traced along the now defined design, inadvertently brushing against Jackie's quivering knuckles and sending a surge of desire through her entire being.

Jackie's breath hitched as she struggled to focus on the woodworking lesson, her mind consumed with forbidden desires for Marissa. Every movement of her skilled hands sent jolts of illicit pleasure through Jackie's body, igniting a fire within her that threatened to consume her.

"Your turn," Marissa's voice was a seductive whisper, and Jackie felt her resolve crumbling under the weight of desire.

As she mimicked Marissa's technique, Jackie couldn't help but imagine those same hands roaming her body, tracing every curve and dip with expert precision. Her own hands trembled as she dared to imagine Marissa's fingers delving between her thighs, sending waves of ecstasy crashing over her.

"Excellent," Marissa purred, her eyes gleaming with pride and something more. "You're a natural."

Jackie's cheeks burned with a mixture of shame and arousal as she forced herself to focus on the task at hand, pushing away the intoxicating thoughts of Marissa's touch. But deep down, she knew that this was only the beginning of their dangerous attraction."Next, let's work on smoothing the edges," Marissa suggested, picking up a piece of sandpaper and demonstrating the proper technique. As she moved her hand back and forth, the subtle friction generated a soft, rhythmic sound that set Jackie's heart racing.

"Like this?" Jackie asked, attempting to mirror Marissa's movements.

"Exactly," Marissa confirmed, watching intently as Jackie's fingers danced over the wood. "Make sure you apply even pressure and keep a steady pace."

Despite her best efforts, Jackie couldn't tear her gaze away from Marissa's lips, which were slightly parted as she offered guidance. She yearned to taste them, to feel their warmth pressed against her own in a passionate, desperate kiss.

Jackie's heart thumped erratically against her ribcage as she forcefully reminded herself of the reality. She was a married woman, and her desires for Marissa were impossible. Her chest constricted with frustration, a tight knot forming in her throat as she fought to keep her emotions in check.

"Jackie?" Marissa's soft voice cut through her

thoughts, concern etched on her delicate features. "Are you alright?"

With every fiber of her being screaming for release, Jackie plastered a fake smile on her face and replied hastily, "Y-yes. Just lost in thought."

Marissa's gentle hand squeezed her shoulder in reassurance, but Jackie could only feel the heat radiating from their touch. "Remember," Marissa said softly, "focus is key when it comes to woodworking."

"F-focus," Jackie stammered, struggling to maintain composure as Marissa's words echoed in her mind. She would have to bury her feelings deep within and lose herself in the art of woodworking – but it would never be enough.

CHAPTER TWO

The sun dipped low in the sky, casting warm hues across the workshop. Shadows danced playfully on the walls as Jackie and Declan stood side by side, inspecting a newly finished piece. The scent of freshly cut wood and varnish filled the air, a testament to their dedication and hard work.

"Looks good, sis," Declan said with a grin, admiration clear in his voice as he traced his fingers along the smooth surface of the table they'd just completed.

"Thanks, Dec. I couldn't have gotten it to look this nice without Marissa's guidance," Jackie replied, her cheeks reddening slightly at the mention of her teacher's name. She knew her brother was aware of her feelings for Marissa and tried to keep herself composed when discussing her mentor.

"Marissa is an excellent teacher, but you've got natural talent too," Declan reassured her, placing an arm around her shoulders. "I'm proud of what we've achieved together in this workshop."

Jackie looked up at him and smiled, feeling grateful for the support he provided every step of the way. They had a unique bond, one that allowed them to understand each other without the need for many words. She knew she could always lean on him when things got tough.

"Hey, Dec, do you think we can get started on that custom cabinet project tomorrow? I want to try out those new techniques Marissa showed me," Jackie said, her eyes twinkling with excitement as she envisioned the intricate details she'd be able to create with her newfound knowledge.

"Of course, if that's what you want," Declan nodded, understanding her eagerness to push herself further. "Just remember to pace yourself."

"Who do you think you're talking to?" Jackie teased, giving her brother a playful nudge, knowing full well that her determination could lead her to overwork sometimes. "I'll take it one step at a time."

"Good," Declan replied, his gaze softening as he looked at his sister. "I just want you to be happy and fulfilled in your work. And if that means impressing

Marissa and becoming the best carpenter you can be, then I'm right here beside you."

"Thanks, Dec," Jackie murmured, her heart swelling with gratitude and affection for her brother. She knew she could always depend on him, and she was determined not to let him down.

As they stood together in the fading light, a sense of resolution washed over Jackie. She would hone her skills and create stunning works of art, not only for herself but also for her family, their business, and the woman who had awakened desires within her she never thought possible. With each stroke of her chisel and swipe of her sandpaper, she would carve out a future where she could stand tall, unafraid to chase her dreams and face the challenges that lay ahead.

CHAPTER THREE

Next morning, Jackie was at the carpentry workshop early. The sun filtered through the workshop's dusty windows, casting long shadows over the wooden workbenches and tools that lined the walls. Jackie's hands moved deftly over the intricate carving she was working on, her fingers stained with the mix of sweat and sawdust. The scent of cedar filled the air, intoxicating and raw, as she focused intensely on her project. She could feel the weight of Marissa's gaze on her, a subtle heat that made her heart race with both pride and desire.

"Is this angle right?" Jackie asked, holding up the piece of wood she had been shaping. Her voice was steady, but her mind raced with uncertainty. This project was important to her, not only for her development as a carpenter but also as a way to prove herself to both Marissa and Declan.

Marissa stepped closer, her blonde hair cascading over her shoulders, eyes narrowing as she assessed Jackie's work. The scent of her perfume mingled with the wood shavings, and Jackie found it difficult to focus on anything other than the warmth radiating from Marissa's body.

"Almost," Marissa said gently, her fingers brushing against Jackie's as she guided her hand, adjusting the angle of the chisel. "Just like that. Now try again."

Jackie swallowed hard, feeling her arousal flare at the simple touch. She tried to concentrate on her work, but her thoughts kept straying to forbidden fantasies involving her teacher. As she resumed carving, a sudden slip of the chisel caused an unintended gouge in the delicate design, marring the surface of the wood.

"Shit!" Jackie hissed, pulling her hand back and staring at the ruined piece in frustration. Her cheeks flushed with embarrassment, disappointment gnawing at her gut.

"Hey, it's okay," Marissa reassured her, placing a comforting hand on Jackie's shoulder. The touch sent a shiver down Jackie's spine, but she did her best to suppress the reaction. "We all make mistakes. It's part of the learning process."

"Thanks," Jackie muttered, though the shame still lingered. She could feel her arousal turning to anxiety, worried that her desires were starting to affect her performance.

"Let me show you how to fix it," Marissa suggested, her voice soothing and patient. She leaned in closer, guiding Jackie's hands once again, their bodies pressed together as they worked to repair the damage. Jackie's breathing hitched, her mind racing with lustful thoughts, but she forced herself to focus on Marissa's instructions.

"See?" Marissa said, pulling back once they had smoothed out the mistake. "Good as new."

Jackie looked at the restored carving, relief flooding through her. "Thank you," she murmured, meeting Marissa's gaze. The blue eyes sparkled with encouragement, and for a moment, Jackie allowed herself to believe that maybe, just maybe, there was more to their connection than just the love of woodworking.

But as Marissa stepped away, the distance between them seemed to grow even greater, leaving Jackie with a sense of longing she couldn't shake. She knew she needed to keep her feelings in check, both for her own sake and for the sake of her mentorship with Marissa. But as they continued to work together, every brush of their fingers, every shared smile, only served to stoke the fires of desire burning within her.

The sawdust filled the air, catching the golden rays of sunlight that filtered through the workshop's windows. Jackie wiped the sweat from her brow as she carefully chiseled away at the intricate pattern she was carving into the wooden table leg.

"Remember to keep your strokes steady, Jackie," Marissa advised gently, standing just behind her and observing her progress. The scent of Marissa's perfume mingled with the aroma of freshly cut wood, creating an intoxicating blend that made it difficult for Jackie to concentrate.

"Like this?" Jackie asked, attempting to follow Marissa's guidance, but her hand wavered slightly, causing a small chip to break off from the edge of the carving.

"Almost," said Marissa, placing her hand on Jackie's shoulder reassuringly. "Here, let me show you." Marissa moved in closer, her breath warm on Jackie's neck as their bodies aligned. Jackie felt a shiver run down her spine, despite the heat of the workshop.

Marissa reached around Jackie and guided her hands, their fingers interlaced as they held the chisel together. Jackie's pulse raced, her mind awash with vivid fantasies of what those skilled hands could do to her body.

"See? Just like that," Marissa said softly, her voice sending another wave of desire through Jackie. They worked together for a few more moments before Marissa released her grip on the chisel, her fingertips brushing lightly against Jackie's as she pulled away.

"Thank you," Jackie murmured, feeling the heat rise in her cheeks as she continued to work on the carving. She couldn't ignore the way her body reacted to Marissa's touch, the way her heart pounded in her chest whenever their eyes met. It was becoming harder to separate her growing attraction to her teacher from her passion for her craft.

"Jackie," Marissa said quietly, drawing her attention back to the task at hand. "Keep your focus. You're doing great."

"Right," Jackie replied, taking a deep breath and forcing herself to concentrate on her work. She knew she needed to maintain control over her feelings, but with each passing day, it became more difficult.

Her thoughts wandered to Marissa's gentle touch, imagining the way those hands would feel on her bare skin, igniting a fire within her that could only be quenched by their union. The fantasy consumed her, making it nearly impossible to finish her work.

"Jackie," Marissa said again, her voice concerned. "Are you okay?"

"Y-yes," Jackie stammered, her cheeks burning with embarrassment. "I'm fine. Just...distracted."

"Take a break if you need to," Marissa suggested kindly. "We all have our off days."

'Thank you," Jackie whispered, setting down her chisel and stepping away from the table. As she moved to the corner of the workshop, she leaned against the wall, trying to regain her composure. She couldn't afford to let her feelings for Marissa jeopardize her work or their relationship.

As Jackie took a few calming breaths, she watched Marissa continue to guide the other apprentices, her grace and poise never faltering. It was this very dedication and talent that Jackie admired most in her teacher – the same qualities that made her attraction so intense and complicated.

Closing her eyes, Jackie promised herself that she would find a way to work through her feelings and remain focused on her craft. But as she listened to the sounds of the workshop and Marissa's gentle guidance, she couldn't help but wonder if her desires would ever truly subside. And with that thought, the conflict within her grew stronger, setting the stage for the challenges to come.

CHAPTER FOUR

Each day, Jackie found herself more consumed by the allure of Marissa's presence. Her teacher's elegant curves and the way her blonde waves cascaded over her shoulders left Jackie breathless. She couldn't help but stare at the swell of Marissa's breasts beneath her blouse or the subtle curve of her hips when she moved around the workshop.

"Focus, Jackie," she muttered under her breath, trying to shake off her thoughts as she measured a piece of wood and prepared to cut it. However, her mind was flooded with images of Marissa, each one more vivid and intoxicating than the last. She envisioned the two of them tangled together in a passionate embrace, their lips locked in a feverish kiss as Marissa eagerly submitted to Jackie's every desire.

"Shit," Jackie cursed, realizing she'd made an error in her measurement. Her hands trembled slightly as she attempted to regain focus on her work, but the fantasies continued to consume her. It felt like a fire burned within her, stoked by each stolen glance at her beautiful teacher.

"Everything okay, Jackie?" Marissa's voice was soft and concerned, causing Jackie to jump slightly in surprise.

"Uh, yeah. I just messed up this measurement," she replied, struggling to keep her voice steady and her eyes away from Marissa's full lips.

"Here, let me help you," Marissa offered, stepping closer. Her body heat radiated near Jackie, making it even harder for the young apprentice to concentrate. The scent of Marissa's perfume filled her nostrils, a mix of jasmine and sandalwood that sent shivers down Jackie's spine.

"Thanks," Jackie murmured, feeling her cheeks flush with color as Marissa leaned in to help guide the saw through the wood. Their bodies brushed against each other, and Jackie could feel the softness of Marissa's skin through the thin fabric of their clothes. A moan threatened to escape her lips as the fantasy of Marissa, bound and blindfolded, begging for Jackie's touch, resurfaced in her mind.

"Good job," Marissa praised as they finished the cut, pulling away from Jackie with a warm smile. "Just remember to double-check your measurements before cutting."

"Of course. I'll be more careful next time," Jackie replied, her voice barely above a whisper as she tried to steady her racing heart. She couldn't help but wonder if Marissa could sense the hunger that coursed through her veins, threatening to consume her whole.

CHAPTER FIVE

After another long day of struggling to keep her focus on work, Jackie couldn't wait to meet up with her best friend, Talia Martinez. They sat at their usual corner booth in a dimly lit bar downtown, the flickering candlelight casting shadows on their faces as they sipped their drinks. The comforting hum of chatter and clinking glasses surrounded them, providing an intimate atmosphere that made it easy for Jackie to open up.

"Jackie, you've been acting weird lately," Talia said, concern etched on her face as she placed a gentle hand on Jackie's forearm. "What's going on?"

Jackie sighed, her green eyes locking onto Talia's brown ones, searching for understanding. "I...I don't know how to explain it," she hesitated, her breath hitching slightly. "It's Marissa. My teacher. I can't stop thinking about her."

"Marissa? You mean that MILF who teaches woodworking?" Talia asked, raising her eyebrows in surprise. "Wow, I didn't see that coming."

"Neither did I," Jackie admitted, her fingers playing nervously with the edge of her glass. "But it's not just a crush, Talia. It's more than that. I have these...fantasies about her. Intense ones, involving bondage and submission. It's like my body craves her, even though I know it's wrong."

Talia leaned in closer, her voice low and soothing. "Jackie, there's nothing wrong with having fantasies or desires. We all have them, and they don't define who we are. But I can understand why you're feeling conflicted."

"I just don't know what to do," Jackie whispered, her heart aching with longing. "Every time I'm near her, I can't help but imagine her naked, tied up, waiting for me to take control. But she's my teacher, and she's straight...and married."

"Listen," Talia said firmly, her eyes filled with compassion. "First of all, you need to cut yourself some slack. Attraction isn't something we can control. And second, you're not doing anything wrong by having these feelings. We both know that fantasies are just that

– fantasies. They don't necessarily mean we want them to happen in real life."

Jackie nodded, feeling a small weight lift off her chest as Talia continued to reassure her. "You're right, I guess. It's just...sometimes it feels so real, like I can almost taste her on my lips."

"Maybe what you need is to explore these desires a bit more," Talia suggested softly, her hand still resting on Jackie's arm, warm and comforting. "Find out if it's really Marissa you want or if it's just the idea of her that excites you."

"Maybe," Jackie agreed, her mind racing with possibilities. As she looked into Talia's understanding eyes, she felt grateful for their bond and the trust they shared. With Talia by her side, Jackie knew she could face the complexities of her desires and navigate the stormy waters of her heart.

TALIA'S EYES sparkled in the dimly lit room, a warm and comforting presence amidst the shadows that danced on the walls. The flickering candlelight cast an intimate glow over their faces as they sat close together on the plush couch, their legs brushing against each other.

"Jackie, I want you to know that you can tell me

anything," Talia murmured softly, her voice laced with genuine concern. Her hand reached over to gently squeeze Jackie's, a silent reminder of their unbreakable bond.

Jackie hesitated for a moment before taking a deep breath, her green eyes meeting Talia's gaze with a mixture of vulnerability and determination. "Talia, I need to be honest with you about something...I've been fantasizing even more about Marissa lately."

"Fantasizing more?" Talia echoed, her eyebrows arching slightly in surprise but her expression remaining open and non-judgmental.

"More than that," Jackie admitted, her cheeks flushing with embarrassment as she recounted her vivid daydreams. "I imagine her submitting to me, giving herself completely. It's intoxicating, and it scares me at the same time."

As she listened attentively to Jackie's confession, Talia's hand continued to hold onto her friend's, offering unwavering support. She could see the conflict swirling behind Jackie's eyes, and she knew she needed to help her navigate through these turbulent emotions.

"Jackie, I think it's important for you to explore these feelings," she said gently, her voice steady and reassuring. "Maybe try some new experiences, see if this is something that really resonates with you. You owe it to yourself to see where your desires might lead."

"But what if I'm just chasing after something impossible?" Jackie asked hesitantly, her eyes filled with uncertainty. The thought of pursuing Marissa seemed both exhilarating and daunting; she couldn't shake the fear that it was a road to heartbreak.

"Sometimes, taking risks is the only way we can truly discover ourselves," Talia replied, her brown eyes shining with conviction. "No matter what happens, I'll be here for you, Jackie. Just remember that your desires are valid and worth exploring, even if they might seem challenging."

Jackie felt a surge of gratitude towards her best friend, and she squeezed Talia's hand in return, their fingers intertwining. The weight of her secret desire seemed lighter now that she had shared it with someone who understood and supported her unconditionally.

"Thank you, Talia," Jackie whispered, her voice thick with emotion. "I don't know what I'd do without you."

"Hey, that's what friends are for," Talia smiled warmly, pulling Jackie into a tight embrace. As they held each other close, Jackie allowed herself to dream of a future where she could explore her desires freely, bolstered by the unwavering support of her dearest friend.

CHAPTER SIX

Jackie lay on her bed, enveloped in the plushness of the sheets that did little to alleviate the swirling storm of hesitations and doubts that clouded her mind. Her fingers traced delicate lines across her own body, each touch igniting a new wave of longing as she imagined Marissa's soft, warm hands tracing the same paths. The mere thought of Marissa's touch sent shivers down Jackie's spine, her skin prickling with anticipation.

But as the heat within her grew and clashed painfully with the reality of Marissa's marital status and straight identity, Jackie couldn't help but let out a frustrated sigh. "Why do I even entertain the idea?" She muttered to herself, her voice heavy with exasperation. Restless, she tossed and turned, trying to quell the fire burning within her as she pictured Marissa's sultry blue eyes locked onto hers, their desire almost palpable in the air between them.

JACKIE SURRENDERED COMPLETELY to the all-consuming fantasy, her hands moving with a feverish urgency as she fed the insatiable hunger within her. She willed Marissa's presence closer, so close that each breath carried the tantalizing scent of her perfume, driving Jackie wild with desire.

THEIR BODIES PRESSED TOGETHER in a frenzy, every curve molded perfectly against the other as their movements synced in a passionate dance known only to them. "Marissa," Jackie moaned, her voice trembling with longing as her fingers explored every inch of herself. With each touch, she could almost taste the forbidden fruit that was Marissa's lips, their sweetness teasing her with unfulfilled promises and igniting an inferno of need within her.

. . .

The internal battle raged on within her, a constant tug-of-war between her moral compass and the all-consuming desire that Talia had ignited. With each attempt to suppress her desires, they only seemed to grow stronger, fueled by the burning fire that threatened to consume her whole.

"Damn it, I can't keep doing this!" Jackie cried out in frustration, her body betraying her as it writhed with pleasure under her skilled touch. In her mind, she pictured Marissa's hands taking over, leaving trails of scorching heat across her skin and igniting a fiery passion unlike any other.

A voice, distant and haunting, echoed in Jackie's fantasy. She struggled to discern if it was real or just another twisted creation of her mind. Suddenly, she felt the crushing weight of Marissa's body on top of hers, the teacher's breath burning against her skin as she whispered, "I'll show you what it means to truly live."

The plea escaped Jackie's lips in a desperate whisper, her body writhing with longing for the phantom touch of her beloved mentor. With each arch and twist, her arousal intensified, fueled by the cruel reminder that this was nothing but a forbidden fantasy. But even in the face of reality, she couldn't deny the overwhelming craving for the real thing, aching deep within her core.

In the midst of her euphoric encounter with Marissa, Jackie gave in to her deepest desires, succumbing to a final, selfish moment of surrender. Her entire body shook and trembled, releasing primal cries that reverberated through the empty room, filling it with an intoxicating symphony of longing and passion.

As the aftermath of their intense passion settled around them, Jackie felt a fierce determination ignite within her. She was no longer afraid of the challenges and uncertainties that lay ahead, for she had finally accepted the truth: she wanted Marissa with a burning intensity. Nothing would stop her from pursuing the depths of her desires and discovering where they might take her. She was ready to dive headfirst into the unknown, fueled by an insatiable hunger for Marissa's touch.

THE FOLLOWING DAY, Jackie sought solace in Talia's warm embrace. She had finally shared her secret with her best friend, and the relief she felt was palpable. The coffee shop's back room felt like a sanctuary from the outside world - a place where Jackie could safely explore the depths of her desire.

"Jackie," Talia whispered softly, her brown eyes full of understanding as she held her friend close. "You need to remember that your feelings are nothing to be ashamed of. You deserve to be happy, and if exploring this side of yourself brings you joy, then it's worth pursuing."

Jackie looked into Talia's eyes, feeling a renewed sense of strength as her friend reassured her. The weight of her longing for Marissa seemed to lessen slightly, replaced by an unshakable belief that she was worthy of love and desire.

"Thank you, Talia," Jackie murmured, tears prickling at the corners of her eyes. "But how do I even begin to figure out what I want? How do I know if this is just a fantasy or something more?"

"Baby girl, there are so many ways you can explore your desires," Talia replied, her voice gentle yet firm. "Have you ever considered reading erotica or attending BDSM workshops? They can help you understand your own fantasies better and maybe even give you some ideas on how to approach Marissa."

Jackie's cheeks flushed a deep crimson at the suggestion, but she couldn't deny the thrill that coursed through her veins at the thought of delving deeper into her desires. The prospect of learning about the intricacies of submission and dominance intrigued her, and she found herself eager to see how they might translate to her relationship with Marissa.

"Maybe... maybe I could give that a try," she admitted hesitantly, her heart pounding in her chest. "I don't know if I'll ever have the courage to approach Marissa, but... I need to understand myself first."

"Exactly," Talia smiled, her eyes sparkling with pride. "And remember, no matter what happens, I'll always be here for you, Jackie. You're my best friend, and I want nothing more than to see you happy."

As they hugged once more, Jackie felt a renewed sense of excitement and nervousness bubbling within her. With Talia's unwavering support, she was ready to take the first steps towards exploring her desires - and maybe, just maybe, discovering the depths of her love for Marissa in the process.

THE SUNLIGHT FILTERING through the window illuminated the workshop in a warm golden glow, casting Jackie's shadow on the wooden floor as she meticulously carved a decorative piece. With each stroke of her chisel, her thoughts were consumed by Marissa - her delicate hands guiding Jackie's own, the scent of her perfume lingering near, and the thrill of their bodies pressed close together.

"Focus, Jackie," she whispered to herself, shaking her head as if to physically dispel the fantasies that clouded her mind. Her green eyes narrowed with determination, a reflection of the newfound hope Talia had instilled in her during their conversation earlier that day.

As she continued to work, Jackie couldn't help but let her mind wander back to their discussion. The suggestion of reading erotica and attending BDSM workshops ignited a curiosity within her that she hadn't even realized she possessed. The thought of exploring this hidden side of her desires made her heart race, her pulse quickening with every vivid image that crossed her mind.

"Hey, what are you working on?" a voice called out from behind her, causing Jackie to jump slightly and nearly lose grip on her chisel.

"Jesus, Talia! You scared me," she gasped, her hand flying to her chest as her friend entered the workshop. A smirk danced across Talia's lips, amusement twinkling in her eyes.

"Sorry, didn't mean to startle you," she chuckled,

walking over to inspect Jackie's work. "This is beautiful, by the way."

"Thanks," Jackie replied, her cheeks flushing with pride. She took a deep breath before launching into the topic that had been occupying her thoughts all day. "I've been thinking about what we talked about earlier – about exploring my desires and maybe... pursuing Marissa."

"Really?" Talia asked, her eyebrows raising in surprise. "What have you decided?"

"I'm going to do it," Jackie declared, her voice shaking slightly with a mixture of excitement and nervousness. "I'm going to read some erotica, attend a workshop or two... just see where it takes me."

"Jackie, that's amazing!" Talia exclaimed, her face lighting up at her friend's newfound resolve. "I'm so proud of you for taking this step."

"Thanks, Talia," Jackie said, a grateful smile tugging at the corners of her mouth. "It's not going to be easy, but I need to know who I am... what I want. And if there's even a chance that Marissa could be a part of that journey, then I have to take that leap."

"Absolutely," Talia agreed, placing a supportive hand on Jackie's shoulder. "And remember, I'll be right here cheering you on every step of the way."

As they exchanged encouraging smiles, Jackie felt an

electrifying mix of excitement and anticipation coursing through her veins. The prospect of exploring her desires and potentially pursuing a relationship with Marissa had never seemed more attainable.

With the warm sun streaming in through the window and her best friend by her side, Jackie knew she was ready to embark on this thrilling new chapter of self-discovery and passion - wherever it may lead.

CHAPTER 7

Back in the woodworking studio, Jackie couldn't help but steal glances at her teacher, Marissa. The way her blonde hair cascaded down her back and framed her sculpted face was mesmerizing. Jackie's heart raced as she watched Marissa bend over to examine a student's project, revealing the curve of her hips beneath her tight jeans.

"Focus, Jackie," she muttered under her breath, attempting to redirect her attention to the intricate wood carving in front of her. But her mind refused to cooperate, instead weaving fantasies about what it would be like to run her fingers through Marissa's silky locks and trace the lines of her body with her lips.

"Jackie?" Marissa's voice pulled her from her reverie,

causing her cheeks to flush crimson. "Do you need any help with your project?"

"Uh, no, I'm good," Jackie stammered, forcing a smile. As Marissa moved on to assist another student, Jackie found herself wondering if there might be more to her desires than simple attraction. She had heard whispers among her friends about BDSM – something about power dynamics, submission, and control, all wrapped up in a sensual dance between partners. The thought sent a shiver down her spine, igniting a fire within her that begged to explore this unknown territory.

"Damn it," Jackie whispered, gripping her chisel tightly and biting her lip. Her thoughts raced with images of being bound and vulnerable, completely at the mercy of Marissa's expert touch. It was a treacherous path to walk, fraught with risks and potential consequences. But the allure of unlocking her fantasies, of giving in to the magnetic pull she felt towards Marissa, was undeniably tempting.

"Hey, are you okay?" asked a fellow apprentice, concern etched on his face.

"Yeah, just lost in thought," Jackie replied, offering a half-hearted smile. She couldn't help but feel torn between her growing desires and the potential fallout of acting on them. There was so much at stake – not only her professional relationship with Marissa but also the possibility of losing herself in the uncharted waters of BDSM.

"Jackie, can I see you in my office after class?" Marissa's voice cut through her internal struggle like a knife, sending a wave of anxiety coursing through her veins.

"Sure," she responded, her voice barely above a whisper. As the minutes ticked by, Jackie tried to focus on her work, but her thoughts continued to spiral, leaving her feeling more confused and uncertain than ever before.

"Fuck, Talia, I don't know what to do," Jackie confessed as she paced back and forth in her friend's small apartment, her hands running through her short dark hair. The tension in her body was palpable, her bright green eyes reflecting the turmoil within.

"Hey, slow down, breathe," Talia said, placing a calming hand on Jackie's arm. "Tell me what's going on." She guided Jackie to the couch, her curly brown hair bouncing with each movement.

"Marissa... my teacher..." Jackie hesitated, her cheeks flushing red. "I can't stop thinking about her, and not just in a 'she's so hot' way. I mean, she is, but it's more than that. These... fantasies are building."

Talia raised an eyebrow, a knowing smile playing on her lips. "What kind of fantasies, exactly?"

"About BDSM," Jackie whispered, embarrassed but desperate for help. "Being tied up, helpless under Marissa's control. It's driving me crazy, and I don't know if I should act on it or just bury it deep down."

"Jackie, listen to me," Talia said earnestly. "There is absolutely nothing wrong with exploring your desires. In fact, it can be incredibly liberating and fulfilling. But it's important to go about it the right way."

"Have you ever...?" Jackie trailed off, unsure how to phrase the question.

"Been involved in BDSM? Yeah, I have some experience," Talia admitted with a confident grin. "It's not something I talk about openly, but I've been active in the local scene for a couple of years now."

"Really?" Jackie's eyes widened with surprise. "You never mentioned it before."

"Like I said, it's not something I advertise," Talia shrugged. "But since you're struggling with this, I'm more than happy to help you navigate the world of BDSM. I'll be your guide and mentor if you want."

"Would you?" Jackie asked, hope shining in her eyes.

"I don't want to do anything stupid or dangerous, but I can't ignore these feelings anymore."

"Of course," Talia said, squeezing Jackie's hand. "I'll teach you everything I know, and we'll take it as slowly as you need. The most important thing is that you feel safe and comfortable every step of the way."

"Thank you," Jackie breathed, relief washing over her. She knew that with Talia by her side, she could begin to explore the depths of her desires without fear, trusting her best friend to light the path forward.

THE SUN HAD DIPPED below the horizon, casting a warm orange glow into Jackie's bedroom as she sat at her desk, laptop open and ready. The scent of cedar from her woodworking projects lingered in the air, mixing with the faint aroma of coffee that Talia had left behind after their earlier conversation. Her heart raced with both excitement and nerves, her fingers hovering over the keys, uncertainty clouding her thoughts for a moment.

"Okay, here goes nothing," Jackie muttered to herself, taking a deep breath before typing 'BDSM for beginners' into the search bar. As the results populated the screen, her bright green eyes scanned the titles, eager to absorb every bit of information she could find. She clicked on an article that seemed promising, diving headfirst into this new and exciting world.

"Jackie, I found a great book for you," Talia's voice came through the phone speaker, interrupting Jackie's intense research session. "It's a Guide to BDSM for Newcomers. It's perfect for someone just starting out."

"Awesome, thanks, Talia!" Jackie exclaimed, feeling grateful for her friend's guidance. "I've been reading articles online, but it's nice to have something more tangible."

"Of course! And remember, don't be afraid to ask me anything," Talia reassured her.

"Actually, I did want to ask you about the potential risks involved in BDSM," Jackie said hesitantly, knowing it was important to discuss but not wanting to dampen her enthusiasm.

"Great question," Talia responded warmly. "There are physical risks, like injuries or accidents, but those can be minimized by proper communication, safety measures, and learning from experienced practitioners."

"Are there emotional risks too?" Jackie inquired, her mind racing with possibilities.

"Definitely," Talia admitted, her voice softening. "Some people might feel emotionally vulnerable, especially if they're exploring new sensations or pushing their boundaries. It's essential to have open communication with your partner and establish trust."

"Okay, I'll keep that in mind," Jackie said, making a mental note of the importance of trust and communication. As she continued researching, her curiosity ignited by the images and descriptions of various BDSM acts, she couldn't help but imagine herself in those scenarios - bound, helpless, and at the mercy of Marissa's skilled hands.

"Jackie, are you still there?" Talia's voice pulled her back to reality.

"Sorry, I got lost in thought for a moment," Jackie admitted, feeling a flush of heat rise to her cheeks.

"Hey, it's okay. This is an exciting journey you're embarking on," Talia reassured her. "Just remember, take it slow, prioritize safety, and don't be afraid to explore your desires. You're going to learn so much about yourself through this experience."

"Thank you, Talia," Jackie replied, her heart swelling with gratitude for her friend's unwavering support. "I'm ready to dive in and see where this path takes me."

CHAPTER 8

Jackie's thoughts were consumed by the idea of BDSM as she worked in the woodshop. Her eyes drifted over to Marissa, her teacher and the object of her desires.

She could almost feel Marissa's strong hands clasped around her wrists, commanding whispers in her ear heightening her senses. The thought sent a seductive quiver down her spine.

"Jackie," Marissa demanded, her voice deep and firm, jerking Jackie abruptly back to reality. Her cheeks warmed as she was caught in the throes of her own desires. "Sorry," she murmured.

"Jackie, focus!" Marissa called out, snapping Jackie back to reality.

"Sorry," she muttered, blushing from being caught daydreaming.

LATER THAT EVENING, Jackie met up with Talia at their favorite coffee shop, eager to continue their conversation from the day before. The aroma of freshly ground coffee beans enveloped them as they settled into a secluded corner booth.

"Alright, so we've talked about the potential benefits and risks involved in BDSM," Talia began, her voice low and serious. "Now, let's discuss the most critical aspects: consent, communication, and safety."

"Okay, I'm all ears," Jackie replied, leaning forward attentively.

"First and foremost, consent is the foundation of every BDSM encounter," Talia explained. "Every participant must give their explicit, informed consent for each activity, and everyone has the right to revoke that consent at any time."

"Got it," Jackie nodded, mentally filing away the information.

"Communication goes hand-in-hand with consent," Talia continued. "You need to have open, honest discussions with your partner about your desires, limits, and boundaries. Establishing a safeword is crucial – it's a word or signal that, when used, immediately stops the scene."

"Understood," Jackie said, her mind racing with possibilities. "And safety?"

"Make sure you educate yourself on proper techniques and safety measures for each activity," Talia advised. "For example, if you're interested in rope bondage, learn how to tie knots safely to avoid nerve damage. And always have a pair of safety scissors nearby."

Jackie listened intently, her eagerness to explore growing stronger with each piece of advice Talia shared.

"Thanks, Talia," Jackie said, her voice full of determination. "I'm ready to take the plunge and start exploring BDSM. I just need your help finding the right opportunities."

"Of course, Jackie," Talia smiled warmly, placing a reassuring hand on her friend's shoulder. "We'll start by looking for local workshops and events – places where you can learn from experienced practitioners and meet like-minded individuals."

"Thank you," Jackie whispered, her eyes shining with gratitude. "I couldn't do this without you."

As they sipped the last sweet drops of coffee, Jackie's heart raced with excitement. Talia's graceful hands moved swiftly as she searched for local BDSM resources on her phone. A secret thrill rippled through Jackie at the thought of all that was to come - a journey into unexplored depths of pleasure and self-discovery. With Talia leading the way, she was ready to experience all the heights of passion and surrender that she had been dreaming about.

THE LANGUIDLY LIT room throbbed with a blend of anticipation and electricity as Jackie crossed the threshold, her heart hammering. She inhaled deeply, seeking to calm her frenetic pulse, and stepped into the chamber. The workshop was rapidly being filled with people - some conversing in hushed tones, others studying the diverse equipment displayed on tables around the perimeter. Every nerve in her body seemed to be alive with excitement.

"Ah, you've arrived!" Talia pulled Jackie into a loving embrace as the familiar scent of roses and lavender filled the air. There was an electric warmth radiating from the hug that comforted her whole body. "I'm so glad you were brave enough to take this momentous step."

"Gratitude," Jackie breathed, her eyes burning with

desire at the sight of a set of floggers glinting in the gentle light. The leather tails shimmered invitingly, and she could feel a wave of excitement and trepidation surging through her veins.

Talia cooed softly, "Everything is as it should be. You can trust me. I'm here to help you explore new heights. We just have to stay aware and respect each other's boundaries. Communication and safety are key." Her voice lingered in the air, a siren call of sensual promise.

“Absolutely," Jackie breathed, her resolve to adhere to the principles of BDSM burning strong.

The class commenced with polite introductions, but it didn't take long for the instructor – a mature woman with cropped silver hair and a certain magnetic aura – to begin laying out the foundations of the craft. As they moved onto practical demonstrations, Jackie found herself entranced by the glimmering rope and delicate knots that were strewn across the table before her. Her heart thundered as she imagined how each length could be used to bind and tantalize.

"So, bondage is something you've been wanting to explore?" Mistress Eris inquired, her lips turning up in a tantalizing smirk as she studied Jackie's reaction.

"Um, yeah," Jackie murmured, her face flushing with warmth. "I'd love to learn more about it."

"Marvelous," Mistress Eris purred, guiding Jackie's

trembling hands to grasp the luxurious lavender rope. "Let me demonstrate a few fundamentals and we'll go from there."

As Jackie moved along, her body delicately mirroring the experienced motions of the instructor, she felt a shiver of passion and delight. The smooth-as-silk texture of the rope slid through her sensitive fingertips, stirring her dormant longings. She couldn't help but admire Talia, who watched her with an alluring grin as if she could sense the warmth that was slowly flooding Jackie's being.

Talia lipped the words, "Doing great," and subtly ran her finger down Jackie's arm, before lifting it in an encouraging thumbs-up.

Jackie shivered at the sudden sensation and murmured a soft thanks. She closed her eyes and let out a breathy sigh, letting her senses sink into the rope in her hands and the sultry knot she was tying.

As the workshop progressed, Jackie felt herself connecting with her fellow attendees. She loved hearing their tales of debauchery, and how they pushed themselves to explore different depths of pleasure and pain. The BDSM community was much more welcoming than she expected, and Jackie's inhibitions began to melt away as she realized just how expansive the world of sexual exploration could be.

Talia caressed Jackie's back as they stepped out of the workshop. "See?" she purred. "You have a certain flair."

"Thank you for being by my side," Jackie breathed, her heart beating faster from pleasure and anticipation. "I'm so eager to discover more and delve deeper into this world."

Talia winked seductively at Jackie, lacing their fingers together teasingly. "You ain't seen nothin' yet," she purred in a low voice, guiding them farther into the night of possibility.

THE PULSATING BASS of the club's music reverberated through Jackie's chest as she and Talia entered the dimly lit space. The air was thick with the combined scents of leather, sweat, and arousal. Shadows danced on the walls, illuminated only by flickering candles and the occasional flash of a strobe light.

Talia purred into Jackie's ear, her lips close enough that the heat of her breath could be felt. "Welcome to Temptation," She cooed, a smirk adorning her lips. "This is where all your desires come to life."

Jackie's emerald gaze, now fully accustomed to the darkness, eagerly took in all the carnal scenes before her. Submissives and dominants intertwined in positions of power, their cries of delight and anguish mixed with the thunderous reverberations of the music.

"Remember, just observe and learn tonight," Talia cautioned, sensing Jackie's rising excitement. "Take it slow," Talia whispered, her voice laced with desire as she watched Jackie's anticipation swell. "We can come back here whenever you're ready to try something out for yourself."

Jackie shivered with anticipation as they moved through the crowd. She was entranced by the Dominatrix in front of her, commanding her submissive partner with each strike of her flogger. The air blazed with sensation as leather smacked against skin; a symphony that aroused Jackie's deepest passions and made her cravings burn brighter.

The husky tones of a woman, dripping with seduction, brought Jackie out of her trance. Before her stood a statuesque figure with raven hair cascading around her delicate shoulders and electric blue eyes that seemed to pierce right through Jackie's soul. "Excuse me," the woman said, smiling invitingly. "But I couldn't help but take notice of your fascination with flogging. Are you a newcomer to BDSM?" She extended her hand, revealing perfectly manicured nails. "My name is Mistress Vivian."

Jackie's skin tingled as Mistress Vivian's strong grip enveloped her own. "Yeah, this is my first time here," Jackie confessed, her pulse racing with anticipation. "I've been to a workshop, but I'm still learning."

"Ah, a tabula rasa," Mistress Vivian purred, her voice like honey dripping from the comb. "There is nothing more exhilarating than uncovering your hidden kinks and exploring what pleases you. Allow me to show you a few techniques that will open up a world of sensual discovery."

Jackie wavered, her gaze searching Talia's for a sign of assurance. Her friend flashed an encouraging wink, and Jackie's desire to explore overwhelmed any lingering apprehension.

The tang of Mistress Vivian's sweat hung in the air, and Jackie wanted nothing more than to lick it off of her body.

The feel of air across her skin, the lightness of body hair tickling her senses.

"I'm in," she murmured, her voice sultry with anticipation.

"Yes, you'll do nicely." Mistress Vivian beckoned them to a clandestine corner of the club. Various implements lay arranged on a table, and she delicately chose a small leather paddle before handing it to Jackie. "Let us begin with something easy." Her voice was velvet in his ear, her fingers tracing lightly down his arm as she spoke.

Jackie's blood raced through her veins as she felt the smooth, delectable leather of the paddle in her grasp. Mistress Vivian's voice was velvet as she instructed Jackie on how to properly wield the implement of pleasure, speaking of communication and consent as a beautiful thing.

"Are you ready?" Mistress Vivian purred, her intense gaze searing into Jackie as she stood before her.

A heady mixture of leather, sex, and musky arousal.

A symphony of arousal permeated the air; the heady scent of burning skin and the sweet aroma of pussy juices that were slowly trickling down her thighs.

An intoxicating mixture of leather, sex, and arousal, as Jackie's own salty musk floods the air around them.

"Yes," Jackie gasped, heat rushing through her veins at the sight of the paddle in her hands, ready to be wielded.

Mistress Vivian's long, dark hair cascaded over her shoulders in gentle waves as she craned forward to watch her paddle strike Jackie's smooth thighs. The erotic sight sent the blood rushing through Talia's veins.

Mistress Vivian's ass rippled with every strike, the rolls of her flesh jiggling as each blow landed.

Mistress Vivian's sultry smile, her full red lips beckoning Jackie's gaze, the curve of each breast visible through the black cotton of her outfit.

As the first strike landed, Jackie's entire body thrummed with exhilaration. The sound of impact, followed by Mistress Vivian's approving moan, sent a wave of desire coursing through her veins.

A heady mixture of leather, sex, and musky arousal.

A symphony of arousal permeated the air; the heady scent of burning skin and the sweet aroma of pussy juices that were slowly trickling down her thighs.

An intoxicating mixture of leather, sex, and arousal, as Jackie's own salty musk floods the air around them.

Jackie's nipples hardened to points as Mistress Vivian's breath washed over them as she leaned in for a nibble.

The tang of Mistress Vivian's sweat hung in the air, and Jackie wanted nothing more than to lick it off of her body.

The feel of air across her skin, the lightness of body hair tickling her senses.

Mistress Vivian's voice was a growl of pleasure as she urged Jackie to "take it like a good girl," the wet sound of flesh striking flesh punctuating each word.

The sound of leather on flesh was sharp with each

stroke, the hissing air between them a precursor to the salacious scene.

The slap of leather against flesh, the red-hot ache in her skin, the erotic pleasure of being controlled by Vivian.

"Good girl," Mistress Vivian praised, her voice low and seductive.

The smooth leather of the paddle against Jackie's supple skin.

The texture of Mistress Vivian's skin was a mystery, the flesh beneath her fingertips was supple yet taught.

The smooth leather paddle in her hand, a luxurious smoothness that makes her want to explore every inch of Mistress Vivian's body with it.

"Now, show me what else you can do," Mistress Vivian purred.

And so, under the watchful eye of her new mentor and her best friend, Jackie began to delve deeper into the world of BDSM, each strike and caress awakening a passion she had never known existed. Her cheeks flashed with a blush of heat, and a gasp escaped softly, as the heat of desire coursed long and deep, curling down her long, lithe legs. With a gasp, she looked down at her own hands clenching and unclenching in white-knuckled need.

CHAPTER 9

Jackie gasped as the leather flogger bit in to her sensitive skin, the slow burn spreading across her back like liquid fire. She throbbed with pleasure as each strike seemed to mingle with the echo of their passionate kisses. The sensation was overwhelming, and she wanted more than anything for the intense heat that bound them together never to end.

Talia brought the flogger down lightly, her breath catching as it made contact with Jackie's skin. Jackie shivered and moaned in pleasure, her eyes rolling back in ecstasy.

"Is this too much?" Talia asked, a seductive smile playing on her lips.

"No," Jackie managed to gasp out between shallow breaths. "It's...it's perfect."

Talia groaned in approval at the feeling of submission radiating from Jackie's body. She raised the flogger again, this time with more force, and let out a deep, satisfied sigh at the cry it elicited from Jackie.

Jackie was taken aback by the sensations coursing through her body from Talia's strikes.

The red leather flogger's thongs struck her back in rapid succession. Jackie's skin flushed rose, hot and throbbing.

Talia's smile was radiant, her lips curled into a seductive grin that radiated sensuality and confidence. She stood strong and solid, branding Jackie on each blow with her beautiful figure. Jackie found herself mesmerized by the contrast between the flogger's impacts with the silky fabric of her lover's black and red cocktail dress.

"Every strike ignited a pool of crimson spittle that would be dispersed by the wind and dissipate before it hit the ground."

Talia's scent enveloped her, a floral musk of jasmine and sandalwood.

Jackie's body radiated with the sweet scent of vanilla and lavender, radiating from her lover's skin. The swell of her chest rose and fell with each labored breath, her chest heaving in time with the rhythm of the flogger.

"the smell of her own bruised and battered skin, the sweat running down the small of her back, the burning sensation of leather against flesh: a heady cocktail of sex and pain."

Her heart raced, her breath quickened, and a warmth spread within her. She found solace in the rhythm of each impact, losing herself in an intense euphoric trance that aroused her to a state of pure bliss. Jackie felt alive in her skin as her body thrummed with pleasure.

"Are you okay?" Talia paused, her eyes searching Jackie's face for any signs of distress.

"I've never felt better," Jackie admitted, a giddy smile spreading across her lips. She reveled in the intensity of the scene, feeling more alive than ever before.

The taste of leather lingered on Jackie's tongue as it slipped out to lick her lips. The taste of leather and the taste of Talia.

Jackie's tongue flicked out and caught a tear that ran down her cheek, taking a drop of her

Her mouth watered as her mind relived the memory of kisses they had shared, and she felt her body temperature rise as she remembered the feel of the leather strap biting into her fleshThe rapid beat of the flogger against her back made her body tense and relax as if it were a heartbeat. The sharp crack of the thongs against skin, the whip's hiss in the air, the sound of Jackie's breath, rapid and excited.

Jackie's skin, punctuated and dotted with red marks from the flogger, shimmered in the golden sunlight as she flailed and fought against her restraints.

"You take such good care of me." Talia's voice was soothing, "I love you so much." Jackie felt warm tingles flood her body, her lover's soft words melting into a beautiful lullaby that washed over her. She felt at peace in the cruel hands of her mistresses, everything centered on the intense sensations emanating from the wounds Talia had left on her body, all of her energy directed towards recuperation.

"We're not anywhere but here... " Talia admitted. Her words poured into Jackie's body. She smiled as Talia pressed against her from behind, caressing her neck and shoulders with gentle hands.

JACKIE FOUND herself eagerly exploring the BDSM community, guided by Talia's patient hand. They attended workshops and classes together, learning about the intricacies of different types of play. Jackie discovered the beauty of rope work, the complexity of sensation play, and the art of dominance and submission.

"Remember, it's all about trust and communication," Talia reminded her one evening as they practiced tying intricate knots. "Make sure your partner feels safe and supported, no matter what role they're in."

Jackie nodded, absorbing every piece of advice her friend offered. With each new skill she added to her repertoire, her confidence blossomed. It wasn't long before she began participating in scenes at the club, both as a top and a bottom, keen to explore the full range of experiences the world of BDSM had to offer.

As she delved deeper into her newfound hobby, Jackie found herself drawn to Marissa more than ever. Thoughts of her teacher filled her mind during her most intimate moments, her fantasies growing more vivid and intense as she imagined the two of them tangled together in rope or exchanging heated glances across a crowded club.

Jackie could feel Talia's hair as she leaned in close to whisper in her ear. Jackie arched her back, a small involuntary moan escaping her lips.

Jackie's skin was silky soft and warm, her flesh yielding to the flogger's bite. Jackie's back moved in time with the rhythm of the flogger, her back arching and arcing with each stroke.

"The leather braided strands bit into the flesh of her back, leaving behind a trail of stinging welts and crimson welt-prints."

"Have you thought about telling Marissa how you feel?" Talia asked one day, catching Jackie lost in her thoughts.

"Maybe," Jackie hesitated, unsure if she was ready to take such a risk. "But I want to be sure of myself first."

"Take your time," Talia assured her, an understanding smile on her face. "You'll know when it's right."

As the weeks passed, Jackie continued to immerse herself in the BDSM community, thriving under the guidance of Talia and the encouragement of her fellow practitioners. She felt a sense of belonging that she hadn't known she was missing, and with each new experience, she grew more certain of who she was and what she wanted.

"Thank you," she whispered to Talia one night after a particularly intense scene, her body still trembling from the aftershocks of pleasure. "For everything."

"Always," Talia replied, pulling her best friend into a tight embrace. "I'm so proud of you."

Wrapped in the warmth of their friendship, an unbreakable bond forged through trust and shared experiences, Jackie knew she was ready for whatever came next. And as her thoughts once again drifted to Marissa, her heart swelled with anticipation for the journey that lay ahead.

THE SCENT of leather filled the dimly lit room, accompanied by the faint sound of chains rattling in the background. Jackie's pulse quickened as she glanced around, her eyes taking in the various scenes unfolding before her. It was a side of the BDSM community she hadn't yet explored, but with Talia by her side, the nervous excitement coursing through her veins felt intoxicating.

"Are you ready?" Talia asked, her voice low and sultry, making Jackie shiver with anticipation.

"More than ever," Jackie replied, the determination evident in her voice.

"Good," Talia grinned, her fingers brushing against Jackie's wrist, sending a jolt of electricity through her body. "Tonight, we're going to find the perfect play partner for you."

As they moved through the crowded club, Jackie

couldn't help but marvel at the array of experiences on display. A woman bound in intricate rope work moaned softly as her partner teased her with a flogger, while another couple exchanged heated glances across the room, their desire palpable.

"Remember, communication is key," Talia reminded her, giving Jackie's hand a reassuring squeeze. "Be honest about your limits and desires."

Jackie nodded, her thoughts swirling with fantasies that had long lain dormant, now eager to be brought to life under Talia's expert guidance. As they approached a group engaged in an intense negotiation, Jackie's heart hammered in her chest, a heady mix of fear and excitement.

"Hi," a woman with piercing blue eyes greeted them, extending a gloved hand to Jackie. "I'm Mistress Lila."

"Jackie," she responded, swallowing hard. "It's my first time... I mean, I'm new to this."

"Ah," Mistress Lila smiled warmly, her gaze flicking briefly to Talia. "You're in good hands, then."

"Thank you," Jackie murmured, her cheeks flushed with a mix of embarrassment and arousal.

As Talia and Mistress Lila began discussing potential scenes and boundaries, Jackie felt herself surrendering to the moment, her fear giving way to an exhilarating sense of freedom. Each question, each careful negotiation, brought her one step closer to unlocking the desires that had haunted her dreams for so long.

"Are you ready?" Talia whispered in her ear, as they finalized the details of the scene.

"I am," Jackie replied, her voice steady but laced with anticipation.

"Trust yourself," Talia encouraged her. "And enjoy every moment."

As Jackie walked towards her chosen partner, she felt a surge of excitement course through her body, her doubts and fears falling away like shackles. She was finally ready to immerse herself in the world of BDSM, her heart pounding with determination as she took the first steps on her journey of self-discovery.

"Let's begin," Mistress Lila commanded, her voice firm yet gentle, guiding Jackie into a realm of pleasure and pain that would forever change her life. And with Talia's unwavering support, Jackie knew she had everything she needed to explore her deepest desires and fantasies.

"Thank you," she whispered once more to Talia, their eyes meeting in a silent exchange of trust and love, before stepping into the unknown, ready to embrace all the possibilities that awaited her.

Hands On Instruction

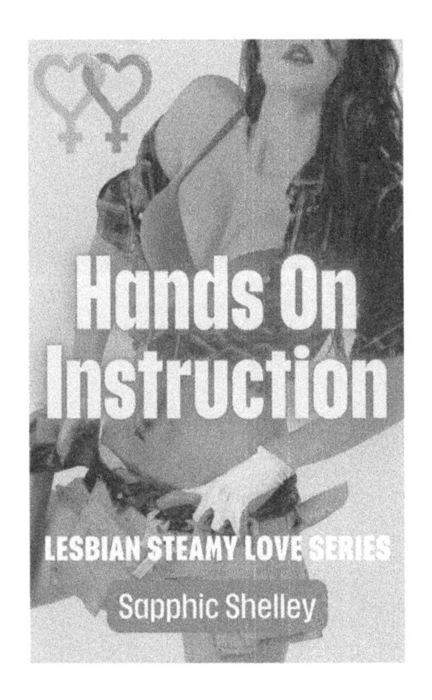

FOREWORD

Nineteen-year-old Jaqueline is a skilled carpenter's apprentice who spends her days crafting beautiful pieces of furniture and dreaming of her MILF teacher. Her persistence pays off, and she finally gets the chance to explore her deepest desires with the woman of her dreams. This story is a bold exploration of sexuality and identity, a powerful reminder that sometimes, the things we want most in life require us to take risks and push beyond our comfort zones.

CHAPTER ONE

Jaqueline, a young woman with curves in all the right places, meticulously traced the rough grain of the wooden plank with nimble fingers. The smell of sawdust and freshly-cut wood filled her small workshop, surrounding her like a comforting embrace. Her thoughts were a tangled mess of desires and fears, but she pushed them aside to focus on her work.

Across from her sat Nina Patel, another apprentice in their carpentry business. Nina's long black hair was pulled back into a tight ponytail, accentuating her sharp features and strong jawline. Beads of sweat glistened on her brow as she honed her craft with intense concentration. Jackie couldn't help but admire the confidence that radiated from Nina – a few years older than Jackie, yet already so skilled and driven.

As they worked side by side, Jackie couldn't shake off the feeling of being both intimidated and drawn to Nina. They shared the same role within the business, both apprentices learning the trade, but Nina seemed to push herself and those around her to excel even further. She was like a master craftsman in training, and Jackie found herself wanting to learn everything she could from her.

Nina's voice cuts through the silence of the workshop, and Jackie jumps, startled out of her thoughts. She quickly wipes her hands on her jeans, trying to mask the tremble in her fingers.

"What's wrong with you today, Jackie?" Nina asks, her eyes sharp as she takes in Jackie's distracted state.

"I...I've just been thinking about some things," Jackie stammers, avoiding eye contact.

"What things?" Nina prods, stepping closer until she's right beside Jackie.

"I don't know if I should even tell you," Jackie confesses, her voice raw with emotion.

"Don't be silly. You can tell me anything," Nina reassures her, but the warmth in her tone doesn't quite reach her eyes.

Jackie feels her heart racing as she takes a shaky

breath, the anticipation of what she's about to reveal making her cheeks burn with embarrassment. "I've been diving headfirst into the BDSM lifestyle," she confesses, her voice trembling slightly. "It's something I've always been drawn to, and I finally decided to embrace it."

Nina's eyes widen in surprise and intrigue at Jackie's words. "Really? That's something that's always intrigued me too. I've done my fair share of research, but never had the chance to truly explore it."

"Wow," Jackie breathes out, feeling a surge of excitement and relief at finding someone who shares her interests. "I had no idea you were into that."

A mischievous grin spreads across Nina's lips as she leans against the workbench, her gaze holding steady on Jackie. "Looks like we have more in common than just woodworking," she teases.

The atmosphere between them crackles with an electric intensity as they both realize the depth of their connection. "So...have you tried anything specific yet?" Nina asks, a hint of curiosity and desire laced in her words as she looks at Jackie expectantly.

Jackie's voice trembled as she spoke, barely audible over the pounding of her heart. "I've been...experimenting with rope play and...spanking."

"Spanking?" Nina's eyebrow raised in amusement.

"That can be quite intense if done correctly. And rope play is something I've always wanted to explore."

The thought of sharing this secret desire with someone she admired caused Jackie's pulse to race. "Really?"

Nina's eyes darted to the door, checking for any potential listeners before returning to Jackie. "Yes, perhaps we could assist each other? Learn together."

A surge of excitement shot through Jackie at the idea of embarking on this journey with Nina by her side. "I'm all in. How about we meet after work this week and see what we can discover together?"

"Deal," Nina agreed, extending her hand. As they shook on it, Jackie couldn't ignore the electric connection between them, wondering where their shared exploration would take them both.

After two days of restless anticipation, Jackie finally found herself standing outside Nina's apartment, her heart racing with excitement. Work had been a blur since their conversation, her mind consumed with thoughts and fantasies of what they might explore together. The door swung open, revealing Nina dressed in a tight-fitting black tank top and shorts that hugged her slender curves.

"Come on in," Nina said, a mischievous glint in her dark eyes. "I've prepared a special space for us to practice."

As Jackie followed her inside, she couldn't help but notice the faint scent of incense in the air. In the living area, she saw that Nina had cleared away all the furniture, creating an open space covered by a soft mat. Her gaze lingered on the various pieces of BDSM equipment carefully laid out – ropes, cuffs, and even a riding crop – each one promising new sensations and experiences.

The air was charged with electricity as Jackie stepped into the dimly lit room, her heart racing with a mix of excitement and apprehension. She couldn't believe she was finally here, about to embark on a journey into the world of BDSM with Nina as her guide.

"Ready to begin?" Nina's husky voice sent shivers down Jackie's spine, her emerald eyes glinting in the low light.

Jackie nodded eagerly, feeling an intense heat radiate through her body as she took in the sight before her - ropes and restraints dangling from the ceiling, leather whips and paddles displayed on a nearby table.

"Now remember," Nina's gaze bore into Jackie's,

"we're going to push your limits but always within your comfort zone. Trust is key in this dynamic."

With a mischievous grin, Nina began to demonstrate various rope techniques on Jackie's willing body, igniting a fire inside of her that she never knew existed. As their bodies intertwined and boundaries were pushed, Jackie felt herself surrendering completely to Nina as her sexy sensei.

Nina's hands moved with a fluid grace as she began demonstrating various knots and ties. Jackie couldn't tear her eyes away, completely entranced by the precise yet elegant movements. Every word and gesture was absorbed by Jackie, eager to learn from Nina's experience.

"Okay, now it's your turn," Nina encouraged, handing the rope over to Jackie. As she fumbled with the knots, Nina stood close, patiently guiding her hands when necessary. Their fingers brushed against each other, sending tingling rushes of electricity through Jackie's skin.

"Excellent work," Nina praised, admiring Jackie's handiwork. "Now let me show you something a bit more advanced." With a mischievous glint in her eye, Nina proceeded to demonstrate the intricate knot with ease and finesse.

As the evening wore on, they delved deeper into the

realm of BDSM, exploring techniques and practices that pushed Jackie to her limits. She eagerly absorbed each new skill, her confidence soaring with every mark she left on Nina's skin.

"Am I doing this right?" Jackie gasped after delivering a sharp strike with the riding crop, her hand trembling with adrenaline.

"Beautifully," Nina moaned, arching her back in pleasure as the sting radiated through her body. "You were made for this, my dear."

Jackie blushed at the compliment, unsure of how to respond. She was grateful for Nina's guidance, but a part of her couldn't shake off the nagging feeling of guilt and uncertainty.

"Thank you," Jackie mumbled, her voice betraying her inner turmoil. "But I can't help but wonder if this is the right path for me."

Nina's reassuring hand on hers only added to the conflicting emotions swirling inside Jackie. She wanted to embrace this side of herself that she had never explored before, but at the same time, she couldn't ignore the doubts and fears creeping in.

As they continued their late night practice, Jackie couldn't help but question everything – her desires, her choices, and even her new mentor. Could she truly trust Nina or was this all just a dangerous game?

CHAPTER TWO

As the warm afternoon sunlight filtered through the workshop's windows, Jackie found herself hesitating at the threshold of a new experience. She stood in front of a large wooden St. Andrew's cross, her fingers nervously gripping a soft leather flogger. Her heart raced as she looked over at Nina, who was patiently waiting for her to take her first swing.

"Remember what we talked about," Nina encouraged gently, her dark eyes locked onto Jackie's. "Listen to your partner, communicate, and most importantly, trust yourself."

Jackie swallowed hard, her bright green eyes flicking down to the flogger in her hand. The weight of it felt foreign, almost intimidating. She had always been confident in her carpentry skills, but this... this was uncharted territory. And yet, there was something undeniably alluring about the power it represented.

"Okay," Jackie said softly, taking a deep breath as she raised the flogger, her arm trembling slightly. "Here goes."

Her first strike landed awkwardly, the tails of the flogger barely grazing Nina's exposed back. Jackie winced, immediately worried that she had done something wrong.

"Hey," Nina reassured with a smile, turning her head to look at Jackie. "It's okay. You're just getting started. It takes practice."

Jackie nodded, her cheeks flushing with embarrassment. She focused on her breathing, trying to calm her racing heart. With each exhale, she let go of a little more fear and uncertainty, until finally, she lifted the flogger again.

"Alright," she murmured, her grip now firm and steady. "Let's try this again."

This time, her strike was more controlled, the tails of the flogger landing with a satisfying thud against Nina's skin. Jackie felt a thrill run through her, a spark of excitement igniting in the pit of her stomach.

"Better," Nina praised, her voice low and sultry. "But I think you can push yourself further. Test your limits."

Jackie hesitated for a moment, considering Nina's challenge. She knew that exploring her boundaries was an essential part of this journey, but it also meant facing her fears head-on.

"Trust me, Jackie," Nina whispered, sensing her hesitation. "You're stronger than you think."

With a determined nod, Jackie raised the flogger once more, her green eyes blazing with newfound resolve. Each strike grew more confident, more daring, as she pushed herself to explore uncharted depths of desire and power. And as she did, she felt herself becoming more alive, more connected to Nina than ever before.

"See?" Nina said with a grin, her skin flushed from the impact. "I told you, you could do it."

"Thank you," Jackie breathed, her eyes shining with gratitude as she looked at her mentor. "For believing in me."

"Always," Nina replied, reaching out to squeeze Jackie's hand. "Now let's see what else we can discover together."

THE WARM GLOW of candles flickered around the dimly lit room, casting shadows that danced along the walls.

Jackie stood in the center, eyes closed, her hands bound behind her back with a soft silk rope. The sensation of the fabric against her skin sent shivers down her spine. She could feel the adrenaline pumping through her veins, her heart pounding in her chest. Her breaths came in shallow gasps as she anticipated Nina's next move.

"Are you ready?" Nina asked gently, her voice low and seductive. Jackie nodded, her body tingling with anticipation. She had grown to trust Nina completely, allowing herself to be led deeper into the realm of BDSM under her guidance.

"Remember, communication is key," Nina reminded her, stepping closer. "If at any point you need to stop or slow down, just say your safeword."

"Understood," Jackie whispered, her voice trembling with a mix of excitement and nerves.

"Good girl," Nina praised, her fingertips grazing Jackie's collarbone delicately, making her shiver. "Now, let's begin."

Jackie felt the cool touch of metal against her skin as Nina fastened a pair of nipple clamps onto her. The initial pinch made her wince, but the pain soon gave way to pleasure as Nina tugged on the connecting chain gently.

"Is this okay?" Nina checked in, gauging Jackie's reaction carefully.

"Y-yes," Jackie stammered, her mind racing as she struggled to process the sensations flooding her body. Each tug of the chain sent waves of pleasure rippling through her.

"Good," Nina murmured, smiling as she watched Jackie surrender to the experience. "You're doing so well."

As the scene progressed, Jackie found herself sinking deeper into submission, her fears and uncertainties melting away with each new sensation. Nina guided her expertly through a range of activities, from the sting of a leather paddle to the exquisite pressure of a pinwheel, each one awakening new desires within Jackie's core.

"Tell me how you feel," Nina commanded, her eyes locked onto Jackie's as she traced the edge of a riding crop along her inner thigh.

"Empowered," Jackie breathed, her voice full of wonder. "I never thought I could experience pleasure like this."

"Remember that feeling," Nina advised, her gaze softening. "It's important to embrace your desires, and understand that there's strength in vulnerability."

Jackie nodded, her bright green eyes shining with gratitude as she looked up at her mentor. She felt a newfound sense of freedom, knowing that she had faced her fears and emerged stronger for it.

"Thank you, Nina," she whispered, her voice filled with emotion. "For showing me this world, and helping me find myself."

"Anytime, Jackie," Nina replied warmly, giving her hand a reassuring squeeze. "I'm honored to be a part of your journey."

CHAPTER THREE

The soft glow of the workshop's overhead light illuminated the workspace, casting shadows on the tools that hung from the walls. Jackie stood at her workbench, carving meticulous details into a wooden sculpture with practiced skill. Her fingers danced across the wood as she etched her desires and newfound confidence into the piece.

"Jackie, you've really outdone yourself this time," Nina remarked, walking over to admire her friend's craftsmanship. She leaned in closer, admiring the intricate patterns that seemed to tell a story of their own.

"Thanks, Nina. I feel like I've finally found my voice," Jackie replied, her bright green eyes filled with pride. Her recent experiences under Nina's mentorship had not only helped her embrace her desires within the

BDSM community but had also given her a renewed sense of purpose in her art.

"Your growth is truly impressive, both as an artist and as a person," Nina said warmly, placing a supportive hand on Jackie's shoulder. "I'm so proud of you."

"Thank you, Nina." Jackie looked up at her friend, her eyes shimmering with gratitude. "I couldn't have done it without you."

"Are you ready for tonight?" Nina asked, her voice tinged with excitement as she changed the subject.

"Absolutely," Jackie responded, her heart pounding in anticipation. Tonight, they were attending a local BDSM event together, where Jackie would put her newly-acquired skills to the test.

As the evening unfolded, Jackie marveled at the sense of belonging that enveloped her. Under Nina's watchful eye, she confidently navigated the various activities, demonstrating her proficiency in the art of submission and dominance.

"Amazing job, Jackie!" Nina praised, watching as her protégé expertly bound a willing participant, weaving intricate knots with ease.

"Thank you, Nina," Jackie beamed, her cheeks flushed with satisfaction. As she looked around the room, she noticed the admiring glances from other members of the community, and her heart swelled with pride.

"Let's take a break," Nina suggested, guiding Jackie to a quiet corner of the venue. They sat down on a plush sofa, their bodies pressed closely together, sharing warmth and comfort.

"Tonight has been incredible," Jackie murmured, her heart still racing from the exhilarating scenes she had participated in. "I feel so alive, so powerful. It's all thanks to you."

"Jackie, I may have guided you, but this was your journey," Nina replied softly, her eyes locked onto Jackie's. "You've grown so much, and it's been an honor to witness your transformation."

"Thank you," Jackie whispered, her voice cracking with emotion. She leaned in closer, resting her head on Nina's shoulder as they shared a moment of connection, their friendship solidifying in the midst of their mutual passion for BDSM.

"Let's go back out there, shall we?" Nina suggested after a few moments, her voice filled with excitement. "There's so much more for us to explore."

"Absolutely," Jackie agreed, her eyes gleaming with anticipation. Hand in hand, they stepped back into the vibrant world that had become their sanctuary, ready to face whatever challenges lay ahead, side by side.

THE FLICKERING CANDLELIGHT danced across the walls, casting shadows that seemed to sway to the rhythm of Jackie's pounding heart. She gazed into Nina's eyes, their faces only inches apart, as their breaths mingled in the warm air between them. The scent of leather and wax filled the room, a reminder of the experiences they had shared, and the bond that had grown deeper with each passing day.

"Thank you, Nina," Jackie murmured, her voice trembling with emotion. "I never thought I'd find someone who understood me like you do."

Nina's hand traced a path up Jackie's arm, stopping at her shoulder, fingers gripping it firmly yet gently. "Jackie, the pleasure has been all mine. Watching you grow and embrace your desires has been an amazing experience for both of us."

Jackie bit her lip, feeling a rush of heat surge through her body at the memory of their recent exploits. They had pushed each other to new heights, exploring the boundaries of pain, pleasure, and trust. Each encounter left her yearning for more, and the anticipation of what was to come sent shivers down her spine.

"Promise me we'll keep doing this," Jackie whispered, her eyes pleading. "I don't know what I would do without your guidance."

"Of course," Nina responded, her voice laced with affection and determination. "We have so much more to learn, and I can't wait to see where our journey takes us."

Their lips met in a searing kiss, their tongues tangling with fervent passion. As they broke apart, Jackie's mind raced with visions of their future adventures. She could already picture the intricate designs of rope constraining her limbs, the sharp bite of a flogger against her skin, and the intoxicating power that came from knowing she was not alone in her desires.

"Let's get some rest," Nina suggested, her eyes shining with the promise of tomorrow. "We have a whole world to conquer, and we'll do it together."

As they curled up in each other's arms, the room fading into darkness, Jackie knew that she had found something special. Her heart swelled with gratitude for the woman who had become her mentor, confidant, and friend. Together, they would face the challenges ahead and continue to grow as individuals and as a team, united by their passion for BDSM.

And with that thought, Jackie drifted off to sleep, her dreams filled with the exhilarating possibilities that awaited them both.

CHAPTER FOUR

The warm afternoon sun bathed the small park in a golden light, casting long shadows across the well-manicured lawns. It was the perfect setting for Jackie and Marissa's first meeting outside of their woodworking class. As they strolled along the gravel path, both women felt the thrill of venturing into uncharted territory—away from the familiar smell of sawdust and the whirr of machines.

"Marissa, I love coming here," Jackie said, her bright green eyes shining with excitement as she gestured at the vibrant flower beds surrounding them. "It feels like such an escape from the workshop."

Marissa nodded, her blonde hair catching the sunlight as she tilted her head up to take in the beauty around them. "It's lovely, Jackie. A much-needed break from our usual environment."

Jackie glanced at Marissa nervously, wanting to broach the topic that had been consuming her thoughts recently. Her heart raced, and she could feel her palms growing damp with sweat. She took a deep breath to steady herself and then plunged into the conversation.

"Marissa, I've been exploring something new lately... something that has really opened my eyes to what I desire," Jackie began, her voice wavering slightly. "I'm not sure how you'll react, but I wanted to share it with you."

Marissa's curiosity piqued, and she turned her full attention to Jackie. "Of course, Jackie. You can tell me anything."

"Okay, so... I've been trying out BDSM," Jackie confessed, her cheeks flushing a deep shade of red. She forced herself to maintain eye contact with Marissa, determined to gauge her reaction.

"Really?" Marissa asked, her eyes widening in surprise. "I didn't expect that. But please, go on."

"Right, so... I've been attending workshops and events, learning about all the different aspects of BDSM," Jackie continued, her confidence growing as she saw Marissa's open expression. "It's been a fascinating journey, and I've discovered so much about myself in the process."

Marissa's eyes held a mix of curiosity and concern. "Does it hurt, Jackie? I mean... some of the things I've heard about..."

"Sometimes there's pain, yes," Jackie admitted, "but it's consensual and carefully controlled. It's more about trust, power dynamics, and surrendering to your partner. And honestly, I feel more alive and connected during those moments than I ever have before."

As they walked on, Jackie noticed the thoughtful look on Marissa's face. She couldn't help but wonder if the seed she had planted might eventually bloom into something more between them.

A WARM BREEZE ruffled Marissa's wavy blonde hair as she listened intently to Jackie's words. Her deep blue eyes were filled with an unexpected curiosity, reflecting her genuine interest in this hidden world Jackie had begun to explore.

"Tell me more," Marissa said softly, her voice tinged with wonder. She leaned in closer, her gaze locked onto Jackie's bright green eyes.

Jackie's heart raced at the proximity, but she

focused on sharing her newfound knowledge. "Well, BDSM is really about building trust and exploring boundaries with your partner. There are different types of play, like sensation play, bondage, impact play... the list goes on."

"Wow," Marissa breathed, her eyes flicking down to Jackie's lips for a brief moment before returning to her eyes. "I never knew there was so much to it. It sounds... intense."

"Intense, yes, but also incredibly freeing," Jackie replied, her excitement evident in her flushed cheeks and sparkling eyes. "The level of communication required brings you so much closer to your partner."

Marissa nodded thoughtfully, her elegant fingers tapping against her chin. "I've always been curious about trying new things, but I wouldn't even know where to start."

"Would you like me to lend you some books or resources? I found them really helpful when I first started learning about BDSM," Jackie offered, her eagerness to share her passion shining through.

"Really? You'd do that for me?" Marissa asked, her eyes widening in surprise.

"Of course!" Jackie exclaimed, her hand reaching out to gently squeeze Marissa's arm. "I want to help you explore your desires, just like someone helped me."

Marissa smiled warmly at her student, feeling a rush of gratitude for Jackie's openness and support. "Thank you, Jackie. That means a lot to me."

As they continued their conversation, Jackie couldn't help but imagine Marissa in various BDSM scenarios – bound and blindfolded, or perhaps wielding a flogger with practiced precision. The images sent shivers down her spine, and she wondered if Marissa's curiosity would ever lead them to explore these desires together.

"Let me know if you have any questions," Jackie said softly, her voice barely audible over the rustling of leaves nearby. "I'm always here for you."

"Thank you, Jackie," Marissa replied, her eyes shining with newfound determination. "I promise I'll make good use of those resources."

Jackie smiled warmly as they walked on, their connection deepening with each step. Little did they know that this conversation would be the first of many, opening doors to uncharted territories and creating a bond that went beyond the walls of their woodworking class.

THE FOLLOWING WEEK, Marissa found herself standing in front of her bedroom mirror, clutching the stack of BDSM books Jackie had loaned her. Her heart raced with a mix of excitement and trepidation, as she gazed at her own reflection. The elegant woman staring back at her, dressed in a silk robe, seemed almost foreign now, her blue eyes filled with uncertainty.

"Is this really what I want?" she whispered to herself, her fingers tracing the embossed covers. "What would John think of me?"

The thought of her husband's reaction weighed heavily on her mind, but the urge to explore her newfound desires was undeniable. She felt torn between the loyalty to her marriage and the need to satisfy her own curiosities.

"Marissa, are you ready?" Jackie called from the living room, her voice laced with anticipation.

"Coming," Marissa replied, taking a deep breath to steady her nerves. She stepped out of her bedroom, her steps light but resolute.

As soon as they were together, Jackie noticed the hesitation in Marissa's expression and took her hand in a comforting gesture. "Hey, it's okay to be nervous. We're just going to observe and learn tonight, nothing more. You don't have to do anything you're not comfortable with."

"Thank you, Jackie," Marissa murmured, her face flushing with gratitude. "I appreciate your support."

In a dimly lit room filled with people, they stood side by side amidst the hum of excited chatter. The air was charged with electricity, the scent of leather and candle wax hanging heavy. Marissa's heart pounded as they watched various demonstrations, each one awakening a part of her that she never knew existed.

"Are you alright?" Jackie asked, her green eyes searching Marissa's face for any sign of discomfort.

"Yes, I'm fine," Marissa assured her, her voice barely audible. "It's just...more overwhelming than I expected."

"Take your time," Jackie advised, offering a reassuring squeeze of Marissa's hand. "Remember, this is about finding what resonates with you."

As the evening progressed, Marissa found herself drawn to a particular scene where a woman was artfully bound in rope, her body displayed like an exquisite sculpture. The vulnerability and trust on display sent shivers down Marissa's spine, and she knew she had taken her first real step into the world of BDSM.

"Jackie, would it be possible for us to attend more workshops together?" she asked hesitantly, her eyes still locked on the intricate knots and patterns.

"Of course," Jackie said, her voice thick with suppressed excitement. "I'd be happy to join you."

With that, Marissa's path was set, and though she knew there would be challenges ahead, she couldn't help but feel a sense of exhilaration at the thought of exploring this new world alongside Jackie.

CHAPTER FIVE

Marissa's pulse raced as she entered the dimly lit workshop with Jackie. The air was thick with the scents of leather and incense, while the low murmurs of conversation surrounded them like a provocative fog. She glanced around at the different stations set up for demonstrations, her eyes widening at the sight of restraints, floggers, and other unfamiliar tools.

"Remember to breathe," Jackie whispered, offering Marissa a comforting smile. "I'm here to answer any questions you have."

Marissa nodded gratefully, doing her best to calm her nerves. As they wandered through the workshop, she found herself drawn to a demonstration of impact play. A skilled domme wielded a paddle, producing sharp, satisfying smacks against her submissive's bare skin. Each strike elicited a gasp from the onlookers, but it was the interplay between the two participants that captivated Marissa the most – the trust, the power exchange, the raw intimacy.

"Is it always this intense?" Marissa asked Jackie, her voice barely audible above the crack of the paddle.

"Intensity can vary depending on the individuals involved and their preferences," Jackie explained, her green eyes sparkling in the dim light. "Some people prefer lighter sensations, while others crave something more powerful."

Marissa bit her lip, considering this as they continued to explore the different stations. At another display, a woman was expertly bound in rope, her body suspended and contorted into an artistic arrangement that left her exposed yet secure. Marissa couldn't help but admire the beauty of the scene, her curiosity piqued by the intricate knots and patterns.

"Rope bondage can be both sensual and restrictive," Jackie said, sensing Marissa's fascination. "It requires a great deal of trust between the partners and can be incredibly intimate."

"Jackie," Marissa hesitated, then plunged forward with her question. "How do you know if this is something you really want to explore?"

"Only you can answer that, Marissa," Jackie replied gently. "But if you're intrigued by what you've seen so far and find yourself yearning for more, it might be worth pursuing."

Marissa pondered this as they moved on, her interest in the world of BDSM growing with each demonstration they observed. And as the evening progressed, she felt a tug deep within her – a desire to delve further into this realm of dark passions and unspoken desires.

"Thank you, Jackie," Marissa said quietly as they left the workshop, her eyes shining with newfound determination. "I think I want to learn more about this world."

"Then I'll be here to guide you every step of the way," Jackie promised, her voice warm and reassuring. And as they stepped out into the night, Marissa couldn't help but feel a sense of exhilaration at the thought of exploring this new world alongside Jackie.

As the workshop continued, Jackie and Marissa found themselves in front of a small, dimly lit room where a demonstration on sensation play was taking place. The air was heavy with the scent of candles and incense, only serving to heighten the charged atmosphere.

"Here," Jackie whispered, "they're demonstrating different types of sensation play - using textures, temperatures, and even pain to create new experiences."

Marissa's eyes widened as she watched a woman run an ice cube along her partner's bare skin, leaving a trail of water droplets that glistened like diamonds in the low light. She felt her breath catch in her throat as she imagined the sensation of the cold on her own body – the shivers it would send down her spine, the way her skin would tingle and her nipples harden.

"Jackie," Marissa asked softly, "do you have any experience with this type of play?"

"I do," Jackie admitted, her voice low and intimate. "I've both given and received sensation play, and it can be a beautiful, intense experience."

"Would you..." Marissa hesitated, feeling her cheeks flush and her heart race. "Would you mind showing me? Just something small and simple, so I can understand what it feels like?"

"Of course," Jackie replied, her voice steady and reassuring. She guided Marissa to a quiet corner, away from the other workshop attendees, and asked her to hold out her hand.

"Close your eyes," Jackie instructed. Marissa complied, her breathing shallow with anticipation. Gently, Jackie traced her index finger around Marissa's palm, making delicate circles that sent shivers up her arm. Then, she pressed her fingernail into the sensitive flesh between Marissa's thumb and forefinger, eliciting a gasp.

"Are you okay?" Jackie asked, concern lacing her words.

"Yes," Marissa whispered, her eyes still closed. "It's just...different than I expected."

"Is it something you'd like to explore further?" Jackie questioned, her breath warm against Marissa's ear.

Marissa opened her eyes, looking into the green depths of Jackie's gaze, and nodded. "I think so. I want to learn more, experience more of this world."

"Then we'll start slow," Jackie said gently, "and I'll be here for you every step of the way."

As the workshop came to a close, Marissa felt a renewed sense of curiosity burning within her, and she couldn't wait to delve deeper into the world of BDSM. She knew there was much to learn and experience, but with Jackie by her side, she felt ready to face whatever challenges lay ahead.

"Let's attend more workshops together," Marissa

suggested, her voice full of determination. "And maybe, when we're both comfortable, we can experiment privately as well."

"Whatever pace you feel is right, Marissa," Jackie agreed, her eyes alight with excitement and desire. And as they walked away from the workshop hand in hand, the possibilities of their shared journey stretched out before them, vast and intoxicating.

THE WORKSHOP HAD BEEN an eye-opening experience for both Jackie and Marissa. As they stood outside the venue, the sun dipping below the horizon painted a canvas of oranges and reds across the sky. The air was cool, yet their bodies still radiated warmth from the intensity of the event.

"Thank you for bringing me here, Jackie," Marissa said with sincerity, her blue eyes shining with genuine gratitude. "I never thought I would be so drawn to this world."

Jackie smiled broadly, her excitement bubbling over as she realized that Marissa's interest in BDSM was more than just passing curiosity. Her heart raced at the thought of exploring this new realm together, and she couldn't help but envision the two of them entwined in a passionate dance of dominance and submission.

"Of course, Marissa," Jackie replied, her green eyes alight with desire. "I'm thrilled to share this part of me with you, and even more excited to see how our journey unfolds."

"Me too," Marissa whispered, a shiver running down her spine as she imagined the possibilities that lay ahead. "So, what do you think we should do next?"

Jackie pondered for a moment, her mind racing with ideas. She didn't want to push Marissa too far, too soon, but she also knew that the best way to learn was through experience.

"Let's find another workshop or event to attend," Jackie suggested, the anticipation evident in her voice. "Something that will allow us to explore our desires a bit more deeply. And, when we're ready, we can take things further in private."

Marissa nodded, her cheeks flushed with excitement. "That sounds perfect," she agreed, her pulse quickening at the prospect of deepening their connection.

As they walked side by side, fingers lightly brushing against each other, Jackie couldn't help but feel a sense of elation. Together, they had taken the first steps into a world unknown, and their shared desires bound them even more closely than before.

"Let's do some research and make plans for our next adventure," Jackie said, her voice tinged with anticipation.

"Deal," Marissa replied, her eyes sparkling with excitement as they locked onto Jackie's emerald gaze.

And so, hand in hand, they strode forward into the night, eager to continue their exploration and uncertain of where it might lead. Yet, deep within their hearts, they both knew that whatever challenges lay ahead, they would face them together, united by their passion and desire for one another.

CHAPTER SIX

The heavy scent of leather and sweat hung in the air as Jackie and Marissa walked into the dimly lit venue, their heartbeats quickening with anticipation. A cacophony of moans and the sound of cracking whips filled their ears as they immersed themselves in the underground world of BDSM. They had both agreed to attend this local event together, following a conversation in which Jackie had hesitantly confessed her curiosity about the lifestyle.

"Wow, this is... intense," Jackie whispered, clutching Marissa's arm for support. The talented young carpenter was used to being in control, her strong hands skilled at shaping wood into beautiful creations. But here, she felt vulnerable, her green eyes wide as they took in the numerous scenes playing out before her.

Marissa, the elegant blonde teacher who had been guiding Jackie through her woodworking journey, smiled reassuringly. Though she identified as straight and had not previously explored such desires, she too found herself drawn towards the fascinating realm of power dynamics and sensual exploration.

"Let's just take it all in," Marissa suggested softly. "We can talk about what we see later, but for now, let's just observe."

Jackie nodded and they began to move through the crowded space, stopping occasionally to watch the various acts unfolding around them. A woman tied intricately to a St. Andrew's Cross, her flesh reddening under the impact of a flogger expertly wielded by her dominant partner; a man suspended from the ceiling by ropes, his body an elaborate canvas of intricate knots; a submissive kneeling before her Mistress, eyes filled with devotion as she awaited her next command.

"Look at that couple over there," Jackie said, her voice tinged with awe. She pointed at a pair of women, one of whom was bound to a wooden chair, her legs spread wide while the other teased her with a feather, brushing it slowly against her exposed, swollen flesh.

"Her control is amazing," Marissa agreed, her blue eyes fixed on the dominant woman's face, which displayed a mixture of concentration and pleasure as she expertly manipulated her submissive's body. "And the trust between them..."

Jackie found herself drawn to the dynamic between the two women – the power, the vulnerability, the surrender. She imagined what it would feel like to be in that position, tied down, with someone like Marissa in control of her pleasure. The unbidden thought sent shivers down her spine and a growing warmth between her thighs.

"Are you okay, Jackie?" Marissa asked, noticing her student's flushed cheeks and shallow breaths.

"Y-yeah," she stammered, trying to force a smile onto her lips. "It's just... I never realized how beautiful this could be."

"Neither did I," Marissa admitted, her voice barely audible over the sound of a nearby spanking. Their gazes lingered on the bound woman for several moments longer before they continued their exploration of the event, their minds racing with possibilities and newfound desires.

THE SCENT of leather and candlewax filled Jackie's nostrils as she and Marissa stood near a corner, taking in the sights and sounds of the BDSM event. She could feel her heart pounding in her chest, both from excitement and nervousness.

"Marissa," Jackie said, her voice wavering slightly as she tried to find words for what she was experiencing. "I... I didn't know it could be like this."

"Like what?" Marissa asked, her eyes scanning the room, lingering on a couple engaged in an intricate rope bondage scene.

"Intense," Jackie replied, her green eyes shimmering with curiosity. "And intimate, even in public. It's so different from what I imagined."

"From what you've heard or seen in movies, right?" Marissa offered a knowing smile. "Real-life BDSM is much more nuanced and beautiful than what's portrayed in mainstream media."

As they spoke, Jackie noticed a dominant couple across the room that drew her attention. The woman wore a sleek black corset, her long dark hair cascading down her back, while the man was dressed in a tailored suit that fit his muscular frame perfectly. They moved with grace and confidence, their eyes locked on each other as if they shared a secret language.

"Look at them," Jackie murmured, nodding towards the couple. "They seem so... connected."

"Power dynamics in BDSM relationships can be deeply intimate," Marissa explained, watching as the dominant woman expertly bound her partner's wrists with silk ropes. "It's not just about pain or control – it's about trust, communication, and exploring one another's desires."

Jackie found herself entranced by the sight, her thoughts racing. She imagined what it would feel like to share that type of connection with someone, to willingly submit to their desires while trusting them completely. The idea both thrilled and frightened her.

"Have you ever...?" Jackie trailed off, unsure if she was overstepping her boundaries with Marissa.

"Explored BDSM, you mean?" Marissa chuckled softly. "A little, but never to the extent of what we're seeing here tonight."

"Would you want to?" The question slipped out before Jackie could stop herself, and she held her breath, waiting for Marissa's response.

Marissa's blue eyes met Jackie's, a hint of surprise flickering across her face before she answered. "I think there's always more to learn and experience in life, don't you?"

The corners of Jackie's mouth curled upwards into a smile, feeling a surge of excitement at Marissa's words. They continued to watch the dominant couple, their hearts racing as they shared this intimate journey into the world of BDSM.

THE HEAT of the room seemed to intensify as Jackie's heart pounded in her chest. She couldn't tear her eyes away from the dominant couple, captivated by the woman's confident demeanor and the way her submissive partner eagerly anticipated her next move. The atmosphere was electric, charged with passion and desire, and Jackie found herself yearning to be a part of it.

"Marissa," she said softly, her voice barely audible over the hum of the crowd, "I think... I want to try this. Submission, bondage... it feels like something I need to explore."

Marissa looked at Jackie, her expression serious yet understanding. "It's not something to be taken lightly, Jackie. BDSM requires trust, communication, and consent from both parties."

Jackie nodded, her green eyes filled with determination. "I understand that. And I trust you, Marissa. I can't think of anyone else I'd rather have guide me through this."

A gentle smile graced Marissa's lips, her blue eyes reflecting warmth and affection. "If you're certain about this, I'm willing to help you explore your desires. But we need to establish boundaries and discuss any concerns or limits beforehand. Your safety and well-being come first."

"Thank you, Marissa," Jackie whispered, her cheeks flushed with excitement and anticipation. "I promise I'll be honest with you about my feelings and any concerns I might have."

"Good," Marissa replied, placing a reassuring hand on Jackie's shoulder. "We'll take things slow, and I promise to listen and respect your boundaries at all times. Remember, this is a journey for both of us, and I want it to be a positive experience."

As they continued to watch the scenes unfolding around them, Jackie felt as if a weight had been lifted off her shoulders. The prospect of surrendering control and delving into the world of BDSM with someone she trusted completely filled her with a sense of exhilaration that she couldn't quite put into words.

With every passing moment, Jackie's curiosity and desire grew stronger. She knew that taking this step with Marissa would change their relationship forever, but she was ready to embrace the unknown and discover the depths of pleasure that awaited them both.

CHAPTER SEVEN

The heavy sound of the door closing behind them echoed through Marissa's apartment, sealing Jackie and Marissa in their private sanctuary. The air inside was thick with anticipation, almost suffocating as excitement crackled between them like live wires. Goosebumps rose on Jackie's skin as Marissa's intense blue eyes locked onto her own, a fiery passion burning within them.

"Are you ready?" Marissa asked, her voice steady and soothing despite the thrill that coursed through her veins.

Jackie could feel her heart beating faster in her chest as she nodded, trying to steady her shallow breaths. "Yes."

Marissa's eyes gleamed in the dimly lit bedroom as she led Jackie inside. The soft music playing in the background only added to the tension building between them.

"Remember, we can stop at any time if you can't handle it," Marissa said, her voice low and seductive. "Just tell me when you've had enough." Jackie's heart raced with a mix of excitement and fear.

"Okay," she breathed out, barely able to contain her nerves.

Marissa's smile turned into a sly smirk as she reached out to tuck a strand of hair behind Jackie's ear. "Let's start then." The ominous promise hung in the air as their first BDSM session began.

Marissa forcefully grabs Jackie's hand and pulls her towards the bed, the mattress creaking under their combined weight. Jackie's body tenses with anticipation as Marissa's fingers trace a path down her jawline, leaving a trail of fire in its wake. Without warning, Marissa's grip on Jackie's wrists tightens, sending an electric jolt through her body.

"Give me your hands now," Marissa commands, her voice dripping with authority.

Jackie eagerly offers her hands to Marissa, feeling the soft leather cuffs quickly secure around her wrists.

The snugness sends shivers of pleasure through her body, igniting a fierce desire within her. With a savage intensity, Marissa orders Jackie to stand up, and she complies without hesitation, trembling with excitement at what is to come.

Marissa's voice dripped with seduction as she commanded Jackie to close her eyes. Anticipation and fear mingled in Jackie's mind as she obeyed, feeling the smooth fabric of a blindfold slip over her eyes. Suddenly, she was plunged into a disorienting darkness, her senses heightened and vulnerable.

"I promise to take good care of you, my dear," Marissa whispered, her breath hot against Jackie's ear. The words sent shivers down Jackie's spine, her trust given completely to this alluring and mysterious woman.

With each touch and caress, Marissa pushed Jackie to new levels of arousal and ecstasy. Her hands seemed to have a hypnotic power over Jackie's body, driving her wild with pleasure.

"Let's explore your deepest desires together," Marissa purred, her words igniting a fire within Jackie that she never knew existed. And as they delved deeper into their sensual journey, Jackie realized that she had found someone who could show her a world of unbridled passion and trust unlike anything she had ever experienced before.

Marissa's strong hand guided Jackie through their first BDSM session, her touch igniting a fire within Jackie's body. With each whispered instruction and gently placed restraint, Jackie felt herself surrendering to the sensations and emotions that washed over her like waves. In this vulnerable state, she found a new level of trust and intimacy with Marissa, each moment reaffirming the deep connection they shared.

As the night unfolded, Jackie willingly followed Marissa's lead, eager to explore the uncharted territories of desire that lay before them. Her body trembled with anticipation as she surrendered to Marissa's spell, knowing that every new experience would bring them closer together.

MARISSA'S VOICE was a feather-light whisper, cutting through the thick tension in the air. Jackie's heart raced as she felt the warmth of Marissa's hand against her thigh, inching ever closer to her most intimate area.

With each delicate touch, Jackie's body ignited with electric sparks, sending waves of pleasure coursing through her. The blindfold heightened her senses, intensifying every sensation and filling her mind with dizzying desire.

As Marissa's fingers traced over Jackie's folds, teasing and tantalizing her with expert precision, Jackie couldn't help but let out a guttural moan. She was completely at Marissa's mercy, overwhelmed by the raw intensity of their passion.

"Tell me if I'm too much," Marissa purred, her voice laced with concern and desire. But there was no going back now, as each stroke and caress pushed Jackie closer to the edge of ecstasy.

Jackie's body burned with desire, her heart pounding in anticipation as Marissa's lips trailed down her neck. Every touch sent electric shocks through her, igniting a fire within that threatened to consume her completely. She gasped for air, unable to control the wild rush of emotions that flooded her mind.

Marissa's words of praise made Jackie feel both proud and vulnerable, fueling the flames of desire even further. As her teacher's hands moved lower, with increasing confidence and skill, Jackie found herself lost in a whirlwind of pleasure and surrender.

Her thoughts spun out of control as she tried to make sense of the overwhelming sensations and emotions coursing through her. She had never imagined herself in such a position, yet it felt natural and right under Marissa's guidance. The trust they had built was unbreakable, and Jackie felt a deep emotional connection blossoming between them.

"Marissa," she moaned, clinging to her teacher as waves of ecstasy washed over her. "I need you... please." The words tumbled from her lips, bared with raw desire as their bodies became one in a passionate embrace.

Marissa's touch sent Jackie into a frenzy, her body writhing with each delicate pattern traced across her flushed skin. Surrendering completely to Marissa's expertise, Jackie lost all sense of self and melted into a state of pure ecstasy. No longer just a skilled carpenter or apprentice, she was now a vessel for pleasure, consumed by the intense sensations that Marissa orchestrated.

"Marissa," Jackie gasped, barely able to form words as she teetered on the brink of release. "Please..."

With expert precision, Marissa continued to manipulate Jackie's body, drawing her closer and closer to the pinnacle of pleasure. "Almost there, my sweet girl," she whispered, her voice dripping with desire. "Just a little more." But for Jackie, the intensity was almost unbearable as she rode the waves of sensation, unable to hold back any longer.

Jackie's body convulses with a force unlike anything she has ever felt before, waves of pleasure crashing through her in relentless succession. She is reduced to a quivering mess, gasping for air as Marissa expertly navigates her through this journey of ecstasy. As the storm begins to subside, Jackie's heart swells with overwhelming gratitude and affection for the woman who has opened her eyes to a whole new world of pleasure.

"Thank you," she whispers, tears streaming down her flushed cheeks as she basks in the intensity of their passion. "Thank you for guiding me through this unimaginable experience, Marissa."

After the whirlwind of sensations had subsided, Jackie lay trembling on the soft silk sheets, her body still humming with the remnants of pleasure. Marissa, her stunning figure draped in a sheer robe, gently removed the restraints that held Jackie's wrists and ankles. Her fingertips brushed against Jackie's flushed skin with a tender touch, sending shivers down her spine.

"Are you alright, my dear?" Marissa asked softly, concern evident in her deep blue eyes.

Unable to form words just yet, Jackie nodded, her chest rising and falling with short, ragged breaths. Her body felt raw and exposed, but also strangely satisfied. Marissa seemed to understand this as she carefully gathered Jackie into her arms, cradling her head against her chest.

"Shhh," Marissa soothed, stroking Jackie's dark hair. "You did wonderfully. Let me take care of you now." The room was filled with the scent of jasmine and sandalwood, adding to the atmosphere of sensual bliss. Outside, the moon cast a soft glow through the window, illuminating the two women in their intimate embrace.

Jackie's heart swelled with emotion as Marissa spoke kind words and wrapped her in a gentle embrace. Warm tears streamed down her cheeks, and she clung to the older woman for support. In this new and exhilarating world, Jackie felt grateful to have someone like Marissa by her side.

"Thank you, Marissa," she whispered shakily, her voice cracking with raw emotion.

"Always, my sweet girl," Marissa replied softly, placing a tender kiss on Jackie's forehead. She guided Jackie to the bathroom, where she carefully wiped away the sweat and tears from her face with a warm, damp cloth.

The scent of lavender and chamomile filled the air, calming Jackie's racing heart. When she was clean and composed, Marissa helped her into a plush bathrobe, ensuring she was comfortable and secure before leading her back to the bedroom.

"Sit down, my dear," Marissa instructed softly, her voice melodic and soothing. She gestured gracefully to the edge of the bed, as if inviting Jackie into a peaceful sanctuary. "I'm going to get you some water and a small snack."

Jackie sank onto the soft duvet, feeling a sense of relief wash over her at Marissa's tender care. As she waited for her partner to return, she took a moment to collect her thoughts. The room was filled with a warm glow from the flickering candles on the nightstand, casting dancing shadows on the walls.

When Marissa reappeared, Jackie couldn't help but feel overwhelmed by the depth of their connection. Marissa handed her a glass of cool water and a plate of fresh fruit, each piece carefully chosen and arranged like a work of art. "Take your time, there's no rush," Marissa said with a gentle smile.

"Thank you," Jackie murmured, gratefully accepting the nourishment. Each sip of water and bite of fruit felt like a small gesture of love and comfort from Marissa. They sat in comfortable silence, basking in the warmth and intimacy of their shared space.

Jackie's heart swelled with gratitude as she looked into Marissa's eyes, filled with a warmth and understanding that she had never experienced before. "I don't know how to thank you," she whispered, her voice trembling with emotion.

Marissa reached out and took Jackie's hand in hers, their fingers intertwining in a strong and unbreakable grip. "Seeing you happy and fulfilled is all the thanks I need," she said earnestly. "This journey we're on is about trust, communication, and pushing ourselves to new limits. And I'll always be here for you, no matter what."

As they shared a plate of fruit, their hands occasionally brushed against each other, sending electric currents through their bodies. Jackie felt a deep connection forming between them, one that went beyond physical pleasure and delved into the depths of their souls. She knew that this experience had forever changed her, and she couldn't wait to continue exploring the intoxicating world of BDSM under Marissa's skilled guidance.

Jackie's lips were swollen, and her skin was flushed as she sat on the edge of Marissa's bed. Her eyes couldn't help but roam over Marissa's body, remembering the intense sensations from their recent bondage session. The power dynamic between them crackled in the air, causing Jackie's heart to flutter with a mix of excitement and nerves.

"Marissa," Jackie spoke up, her voice trembling slightly, "I want to continue exploring this with you, but I need to make sure we're both on the same page."

Marissa smiled reassuringly and reached out to brush her fingers along Jackie's arm. "Of course, Jackie. What would you like to try next? Are there any boundaries or limits you want to discuss?"

Jackie took a deep breath and gathered her thoughts before responding. "I'm interested in exploring more restraint and sensation play... maybe some impact play as well, like spanking or flogging."

Marissa's hazel eyes sparkled with excitement as she leaned in towards Jackie. "I've been thinking about some new possibilities for our sessions," she said with a smile, her hand lightly brushing against Jackie's. Jackie's green eyes lit up with curiosity and anticipation.

"As we explore these new ideas, I want you to know that your boundaries and comfort are my top priority," Marissa continued earnestly. "Please don't hesitate to let me know if anything makes you uncomfortable or if there are things you'd like us to avoid."

Jackie's expression turned serious as she met Marissa's gaze. "I have a few hard limits that I want to establish from the start," she said firmly. "No choking or breath play, and I'm not into humiliation either."

"Thank you for letting me know, those boundaries are important and will be respected," Marissa replied, nodding in understanding. "For me, I have to maintain discretion about our relationship outside of our private sessions due to my marriage. And as your teacher, it's crucial we keep our interactions professional in front of others."

"I completely understand and respect your boundaries as well," Jackie affirmed, appreciating their open conversation and the trust it was building between them.Marissa's hand gently squeezed Jackie's shoulder as she gave her a reassuring smile. "Just remember, communication is key in our sessions," she said, gesturing to the contract they had just signed. "We'll always check in with each other before and after, making sure we're both comfortable and happy."

Jackie nodded, feeling grateful for Marissa's guidance. She took a deep breath and met Marissa's intense gaze. "I want this to be a positive experience for both of us," she said firmly, finding her confidence.

"Trust and honesty are crucial in our dynamic," Marissa murmured, leaning in closer until her lips were practically brushing against Jackie's ear. "And I have no doubt that we will bond deeply through our exploration together." Her alluring tone sent electricity coursing through Jackie's body.

As they concluded their conversation, Jackie felt a sense of excitement and anticipation bubbling inside her. She knew that with Marissa by her side, she was ready to embark on a thrilling journey into the world of BDSM, exploring the depths of desire and trust together.

FORBIDDEN FRUIT

FOREWORD

Young, and curvy woman, lesbian Jaqueline, is a talented carpenter's apprentice who spends her days fantasizing about her attractive teacher. Her determination pays off when she is finally able to fulfill her deepest desires with the milf woman she has been longing for. This story delves into the complexities of steamy romance sexuality and BDSM self-discovery, reminding us that sometimes, achieving our greatest desires means taking risks and stepping out of our comfort zones.

CHAPTER ONE

The sharp, pungent scent of freshly sawed wood and the lingering musk of sweat filled Marissa's small office, a testament to the intense woodworking class that had just ended. Jackie leaned against the door as it clicked shut, her heart pounding in her chest and her emerald green eyes scanning Marissa's face for any hint of discomfort. She had requested a private conversation with her teacher, knowing that what she was about to say would drastically change their dynamic.

Marissa stood before Jackie, her expression a mix of curiosity and concern as she listened to her hesitant words.

"Marissa," Jackie began, her voice quivering slightly but determined to reveal her true feelings. "There's something personal I've been wanting to talk to you about." The tension between them was palpable as the weight of those words hung in the air.

The corners of Marissa's mouth twitched, an unspoken question in her eyes. But she simply nodded, folding her arms across her chest and tilting her head, giving Jackie her full attention.

"I... I've felt this... attraction towards you since I first joined your class," Jackie confessed, her cheeks growing warm with embarrassment but unwilling to hold back any longer. "And it's not just physical. You're so knowledgeable and passionate about what you do, and I can't help but be drawn to that."

As the words spilled out, Jackie could feel her heart pounding against her ribcage. She risked a glance at Marissa, whose eyes had widened slightly in surprise. But she remained silent, allowing Jackie to continue pouring out her feelings.

With trembling hands, Jackie clutched the edge of her shirt as she struggled to confess her true desires. Her heart pounded in her chest, her breaths coming quick and shallow as she awaited Marissa's response. She braced herself for the potential risks and consequences - the blurred lines of their professional relationship, the judgments from others - but she couldn't deny her yearning any longer.

"Recently, I discovered that my desires go beyond a simple attraction," Jackie finally spoke, her voice barely above a whisper. "I've realized that I want... I need to explore a BDSM relationship with you."

The air seemed to still as Jackie's words hung between them, heavy and loaded with vulnerability. Marissa's expression was a mix of surprise and uncertainty, her own hands fidgeting nervously.

"Jackie," she said softly, struggling to find the right words. "I'm... I don't know what to say." But in that moment, Jackie could see the spark of curiosity in Marissa's eyes, and she knew that this was only the beginning of their exploration together.

Jackie's emerald green eyes glistened with unshed tears as she pleaded with Marissa. Her voice trembled with emotion as she poured out her heart, unable to ignore her feelings any longer. It was a daunting request, but she couldn't keep quiet any longer. She could feel herself tearing apart inside.

Marissa reached out and placed a comforting hand on Jackie's shoulder, her own words gentle and hesitant. Her mind raced as she tried to process the unexpected confession from one of her students. She needed time to sort through her thoughts and feelings.

"Take all the time you need," Jackie whispered, trying to sound understanding and supportive even as fear clenched at her heart like a vice. She held her breath, waiting for Marissa's response.

MARISSA'S CHEST TIGHTENED, her heart racing as she tried to wrap her mind around Jackie's confession. The warmth of Jackie's body pressed against her own sent a shiver down Marissa's spine. She could feel the heat radiating from their point of contact where her hand rested on Jackie's shoulder. Her nostrils filled with the faint scent of freshly cut wood and the sharp tang of sawdust that clung to Jackie, a testament to their shared passion for woodworking.

"Jackie," Marissa said, her voice barely audible as her emotions threatened to overwhelm her. The words caught in her throat as she gazed into Jackie's eyes, searching for some sign of understanding. "I... I can't deny that there's something between us," she admitted, feeling the weight of guilt settle heavily on her shoulders. "But I have to consider my marriage. My commitment to Leo..." She trailed off, her fingers digging into Jackie's shoulder, betraying her turmoil and inner conflict.

Jackie's hands trembled as she pleaded, her eyes desperately searching Marissa's face for any sign of hope. Marissa hesitated, caught between her feelings for Jackie and her commitment to her marriage. Before she could respond, the door to her office flew open abruptly. Leo barged in, his usually neat appearance disheveled and his glasses askew. Confusion and suspicion etched across his face as he took in the unexpected scene before him.

"Marissa? What is going on here?" Leo demanded, his gaze already narrowing as it darted between his wife and Jackie.

Marissa's cheeks flushed as she hastily stepped away from Jackie, removing her hand from the younger woman's shoulder. She could feel her husband Leo's piercing gaze on them, and she knew she had to think fast. "It's not what you think," she said, hoping her voice didn't betray her panic.

"Jackie was just discussing some... personal issues with me," Marissa continued, trying to sound calm and collected. "She needed someone to talk to."

Leo raised an eyebrow skeptically, his eyes lingering on Jackie's tear-streaked face. Marissa could see the confusion and concern in his expression. "Is everything okay?" he asked, his tone softening.

"It's nothing for you to worry about," Marissa replied, determined to protect both herself and Jackie from any potential fallout.

Leo studied her for a moment before turning to Jackie. "If you need anything, you know I'm here for you too," he said sincerely.

Marissa breathed a sigh of relief as Jackie nodded gratefully at him. She knew she had dodged a bullet this time, but she couldn't help feeling guilty for involving Jackie in their marital problems.

Marissa's voice wavered as she replied, her words dripping with forced nonchalance. Her eyes darted to Jackie, silently pleading for support.

Jackie's shoulders slumped and her eyes fell to the ground as she struggled to keep her composure. She wanted to be there for Marissa, but it felt like an impossible task in that moment.

Leo's gaze bore into the two women with suspicion, his arms crossed over his chest. But as Marissa continued to speak, his expression softened slightly, as if he were reluctantly being swayed by her words.

"Fine," he finally grumbled, breaking the tense silence. "I'll leave you two to sort things out. Just don't forget about our plans for dinner tonight."

Marissa gave a shaky nod, her fake smile still plastered on her face. As Leo closed the door behind him, she sank onto her desk chair, feeling overwhelmed by everything that had just transpired. Each breath felt heavy and labored as she tried to process the weight of their conversation and what it could mean for her friendship with Jackie.

Marissa's heart raced as she looked into Jackie's tear-filled eyes. "I'm so sorry," she whispered regretfully, her voice barely above a whisper. Her fingers trembled as she reached out to touch Jackie's hand, but she pulled back at the last second.

"I can't just throw away my marriage," Marissa continued, her gaze filled with anguish. "But I don't want to hurt you either. I need time to think."

Jackie nodded silently, understanding the weight of Marissa's words. "Take all the time you need," she murmured softly. "Just know that I'll be waiting for your decision, whatever it may be."

As Jackie turned to leave the office, Marissa couldn't help but feel torn between her desire for Jackie and the guilt of potentially destroying her own marriage. She knew that the choice she was about to make would have long-lasting consequences for both herself and Jackie – and their relationship.

CHAPTER
TWO

"Jackie, can you hand me the chisel?" Marissa asked, her voice barely above a whisper as she stood beside her workbench. The tension in the room was palpable, and she could feel Leo's piercing gaze on her from the doorway of her office.

"Here," Jackie responded, placing the tool in Marissa's outstretched hand. Her touch lingered for a moment longer than necessary, sending a shiver down Marissa's spine that she quickly tried to suppress.

"Alright, what the hell is going on here?" Leo finally exploded, his voice booming through the small space. "I heard what you were saying in there, and it sure as hell didn't sound like something innocent."

"Leo, please," Marissa implored, setting the chisel

back on her workbench as she turned to face him. "It's not what you think. We were just discussing a project we're working on."

"Really?" Leo sneered, crossing his arms over his chest as he glared at the two women. "Because it sounded to me like you were talking about something a lot more personal than woodworking."

"Nothing happened, I promise," Marissa insisted, her hands wringing together as her blue eyes bore into Leo's, desperate for him to believe her. "We were just having a private conversation, that's all."

"Private, huh?" Leo scoffed, turning his attention to Jackie. "You've got some nerve coming onto my wife like that. What kind of sick game are you playing?"

"Look, I'm sorry," Jackie stammered, her green eyes wide with fear as she took a step back. "I didn't mean for anyone to get hurt. It was just a stupid crush, okay? I never thought anything would come of it."

"Damn right, nothing will come of it," Leo growled, his anger barely contained. "You stay the hell away from my wife."

"Leo, enough!" Marissa interjected, stepping between her husband and apprentice. "I don't want you to speak to Jackie like that. She's young and confused, but she didn't do anything wrong. I'm the one who should have put a stop to the conversation before it went too far."

"Marissa..." Jackie murmured, her heart swelling with gratitude for her teacher's intervention. But as she glanced at Marissa, she could see the pain etched on her face and the internal struggle she was enduring.

"Fine," Leo spat, his eyes narrowing as he stared at the two women. "But this better be the last I hear of this, or there will be consequences."

As Leo stormed out of the workshop, Marissa took a deep, shaky breath and looked at Jackie. Her eyes held a mix of sadness and longing, and in that moment, Jackie understood the depth of the turmoil Marissa was experiencing.

"Thank you," Jackie whispered, giving her mentor a small, appreciative smile. "But I think it's best if we keep our distance for a while. Just until things cool down."

"Of course," Marissa agreed, nodding solemnly. "I hope you understand."

Jackie nodded, her heart heavy with the knowledge that their relationship had been irreversibly changed. As they returned to their work, each lost in their own thoughts, the silence between them spoke volumes about the complexities of desire and loyalty that now hung in the air.

THE AIR in the workshop was thick with tension, the whirr of machinery and the scent of freshly cut wood filling Jackie's senses. She couldn't shake the feeling that she was being watched as she worked on her project, her once nimble fingers now fumbling with the tools in agitation. Her mind raced, trying to figure out who had betrayed her trust and told Leo about her desires.

"Jackie," a familiar voice called out softly from behind her. She turned to see Avery, a fellow apprentice and someone she had considered a close friend within the BDSM community. Avery's eyes were filled with a guilty unease, her hands fidgeting at her sides.

"Did you do it?" Jackie asked bluntly, her green eyes boring into Avery's, demanding an answer.

Avery hesitated for a moment before nodding slowly. "Yes, I told Leo about your feelings for Marissa and... your interest in BDSM."

"Damn it, Avery! Why?!" Jackie hissed, the hurt in her voice unmistakable. She clenched her fists, anger and betrayal coursing through her veins.

"Because I'm jealous, okay?" Avery admitted, her own voice trembling. "I've always been attracted to you, Jackie. And when I saw how close you were getting to

Marissa, I couldn't stand it. I wanted to sabotage it somehow, so I told Leo."

"Is this what you wanted, then?" Jackie spat, tears pricking at the corners of her eyes. "To ruin my relationship with Marissa, to make sure I'm as miserable as you are?"

"Jackie, I..." Avery began, but Jackie cut her off.

"Save it," she growled, her chest heaving with emotion. "You've done enough damage. I trusted you as a friend, as a confidant. But you've proven yourself unworthy of that trust."

As Jackie turned away, she couldn't help but let out a bitter laugh. The irony of the situation was not lost on her – in Avery's attempt to bring them closer, she had only succeeded in pushing Jackie further away.

"Goodbye, Avery," Jackie whispered, wiping at the tears that now streaked her cheeks. "I hope you find what you're looking for someday."

And with that, Jackie walked away from her former friend, her heart heavy with the knowledge that the ally she had once cherished had been the one to betray her deepest desires.

JACKIE'S HEART pounded in her chest, a mix of anger and hurt coursing through her veins as she watched Avery disappear from her sight. The cold metal of the chain-link fence bit at her fingers as she gripped it for support, staring out at the empty lot where the BDSM community would often gather. The once comforting space now held only betrayal and pain.

"Jackie?" Marissa's soft voice broke through her thoughts, and she turned to see her teacher standing nearby, concern etched on her beautiful face.

"Marissa," Jackie whispered, her voice catching. "I'm sorry you got dragged into this mess."

"Hey," Marissa said gently, stepping closer and placing a comforting hand on Jackie's shoulder. The warmth of her touch sent shivers down Jackie's spine, igniting the familiar desire that had been plaguing her since their first encounter. "This isn't your fault. I don't blame you for any of this."

Jackie looked away, unable to meet Marissa's compassionate gaze. "I shouldn't have let myself get so close to you. It was selfish of me to put our relationship at risk like that."

"Jackie, listen to me." Marissa cupped Jackie's face, forcing her to look up. Their eyes locked together, the intensity of Marissa's stare piercing through her very soul. "What we have... it's special. It's not something either of us should feel guilty about."

"But you're married, Marissa," Jackie protested, her eyes filling with tears. "I can't keep doing this to you, to Leo. It's not fair to either of you."

"Jackie" – Marissa's voice cracked with emotion – "I've never felt this way about anyone before. You've awakened something inside me that I didn't even know existed. And I can't just ignore it."

"Marissa, please," Jackie whispered, her heart aching at the sight of the older woman's inner turmoil. "I don't want you to throw away your marriage because of me."

"Let me figure this out." Marissa's eyes searched Jackie's, tears glistening in their depths. "Just... give me some time to think and process everything, okay?"

Jackie hesitated, torn between her love for Marissa and the knowledge that their relationship could potentially destroy the life she had built with Leo. But as she stared into Marissa's pleading eyes, she knew she couldn't walk away from her – not yet.

"Okay," she agreed softly, her voice barely audible over the howling wind. "Take all the time you need."

"Thank you," Marissa breathed, relief washing over her features. She leaned in, pressing her lips against

Jackie's forehead in a tender kiss that sent shivers down her spine. "I promise I'll figure this out. For both of us."

As Marissa walked away, leaving Jackie standing alone in the cold darkness, she couldn't help but wonder if they would ever find a way to make their forbidden love work – or if the cost would simply be too high.

CHAPTER
THREE

Marissa's fingers traced the carved wood owl perched on her desk. The detailed feathers seemed to come alive under her touch, a testament to Jackie's extraordinary talent. As she sat alone in her office, Marissa's thoughts swirled, torn between loyalty to Leo and her undeniable feelings for Jackie. The air felt thick with tension, making it difficult to breathe.

"Marissa, we need to talk," Leo said, his voice breaking the silence as he stepped into the room. She could see the hurt and suspicion in his eyes, darkened by a storm of emotions.

"Leo, I..."

"Tell me what's going on between you and Jackie,"

he demanded, cutting her off. His hands clenched into fists at his sides, betraying the fury boiling beneath the surface.

"Nothing's going on, Leo. We're just friends, nothing more," Marissa said, trying to sound convincing. But as the words left her lips, she couldn't deny the electric current that pulsed between them whenever they were together.

"Friends don't look at each other the way you two do," Leo retorted, his gaze unyielding. "I've seen the way she looks at you, and the way you look back."

"Jackie is my student, and yes, we've become close, but it's not what you think." Marissa's heart pounded in her chest, betraying the truth her words tried to conceal.

"Then prove it," Leo said coldly, stepping closer to her. "Cut ties with Jackie. If she means nothing to you, it shouldn't be a problem."

Marissa hesitated, her mind racing. She knew what she wanted – the thrill of submission, the taste of Jackie's lips, the passion that consumed her in Jackie's arms. But was it worth sacrificing everything she had built with Leo?

"Is that your final word, Leo?" she asked, her voice trembling.

"Either cut ties with Jackie or face the consequences," he replied, his eyes unwavering.

Marissa took a deep breath, her thoughts racing as she weighed her options. The idea of losing Jackie was unbearable, but the thought of destroying her marriage overwhelmed her with guilt and fear. She knew that whatever decision she made would change her life forever.

"Alright, Leo," Marissa said finally, her voice barely audible. "I'll do it."

"Good," Leo responded, his face softening slightly. "I just want what's best for us, Marissa. You know that, right?"

"I know," she whispered, trying to hold back the tears that threatened to fall.

As Leo left the room, Marissa sank into her chair, the weight of her decision crushing her. She couldn't help but feel like she had betrayed not only herself but also Jackie, who had shown her a world of desire she never knew existed. Faced with the painful reality of her choice, Marissa wondered if she would ever be able to mend the shattered pieces of her heart.

In the dimly lit office, the scent of sawdust and freshly oiled wood still clung to the air. Marissa's heart raced as footsteps echoed outside her door, each step a reminder of the choice she had made. The heavy door creaked open, revealing Jackie in the doorway, her green eyes filled with a mix of hope and uncertainty.

"Marissa," Jackie said softly, biting her lower lip as she stepped inside. "Can we talk?"

"Of course," Marissa replied, her voice barely a whisper. Her chest tightened at the sight of Jackie's exposed collarbone, her dark hair tousled in a way that made Marissa's hands ache to touch it.

"Look, I know things got... complicated between us," Jackie began, her fingers nervously fiddling with a loose button on her shirt. "But I can't just walk away without knowing how you feel."

Marissa swallowed hard, her eyes never leaving Jackie's. She wanted to reach out, to pull Jackie close and lose herself in their shared desire. But she knew the consequences of that choice all too well.

"Jackie, I –" Marissa started, only to be silenced by Jackie's hand on her thigh. The heat from her touch sent shivers down Marissa's spine, making it difficult to focus on anything but the electric sensation coursing through her body.

"Marissa, please," Jackie murmured, leaning in closer. "Tell me what you want."

Marissa's breath caught in her throat as she felt Jackie's lips brush against her ear, a sultry whisper escaping them. Her mind raced, torn between her loyalty to Leo and the intoxicating allure of the woman before her.

"Jackie, I..." Marissa hesitated, her words dying on her lips as she looked into those haunting green eyes. It was then that the door swung open once again, revealing an unexpected visitor.

"Marissa!" Leo's voice boomed through the room, his face flushed with anger. "What the hell is going on here?"

Jackie's hand withdrew from Marissa's thigh as if burned, and she quickly stepped back, her eyes wide with shock.

"Leo, this isn't –" Marissa tried to explain, panic rising in her chest.

"Save it," Leo spat, his gaze locked on Jackie. "You've made your choice, Marissa. Now live with the consequences."

The door slammed shut behind him, leaving Marissa and Jackie alone in the suffocating silence of the office. Marissa stared at the closed door, her heart pounding in her chest as the weight of her decision settled heavily upon her.

"Marissa?" Jackie whispered, her voice trembling. "What did he mean by 'choice'? What have you done?"

As the truth hung in the air between them, Marissa realized there was no turning back. With a heavy heart, she braced herself for the fallout of what would come next.

CHAPTER
FOUR

The workshop was dimly lit, the smell of fresh wood shavings lingering in the air. Marissa leaned against a workbench, her long blonde hair cascading over her shoulders like a golden waterfall. She shifted her weight from one foot to the other, clearly uncomfortable with the conversation they were about to have. Jackie approached her cautiously, her heart pounding in both fear and anticipation.

"Marissa," Jackie began, her voice wavering slightly. "I know this isn't easy for either of us, but I need you to understand something." She took a deep breath, steadying herself. "I am absolutely determined to make this work between us."

Marissa looked up at her, eyes wide and vulnerable. For a moment, neither of them spoke. The only sounds in the room were the distant hum of machinery and their own shallow breaths.

"Jackie... I appreciate your dedication," Marissa said, hesitating. "But I'm just not sure if I can fully embrace this lifestyle. I mean, BDSM? It's so intense, emotionally and physically. I don't even know where to begin."

Jackie reached out, gently taking Marissa's hand in her own. The simple touch sent electric shocks through her body, igniting something primal within her. She knew she had to be patient, to help Marissa navigate these uncharted waters – but it wasn't easy.

"Listen," Jackie whispered, her green eyes locking onto Marissa's blue ones with unwavering intensity. "We don't have to dive in headfirst. We can take our time, figuring out what we both enjoy and what our limits are. This is about trust and communication, Marissa. We'll find our way together."

Marissa bit her lip, weighing her options. Her mind raced with images of leather cuffs, blindfolds, and silk ropes – enticing yet terrifying all at once. She knew that Jackie was right, that this was a journey they needed to embark on together. But the thought of surrendering control, of giving herself over to another person so completely... it made her stomach twist in knots.

"Jackie, I..." Marissa's voice cracked, and she trailed off. She looked down at their clasped hands, feeling a strange warmth spread through her body. As much as she wanted to deny it, there was something about Jackie – her confidence, her passion, her undeniable magnetism – that drew her in like a moth to a flame.

"Marissa, please trust me. I will be here for you every step of the way," Jackie reassured, her thumb gently caressing Marissa's knuckles. "Let me help you explore this side of yourself, this world that we can create together."

Marissa stared deep into Jackie's eyes, searching for any hint of insincerity or doubt. All she found was unwavering determination and love. With a shaky exhale, she nodded her head, signaling her willingness to take the first steps into the unknown.

"Alright, Jackie," she whispered, squeezing her hand tightly. "I'll try. For us."

A smile bloomed on Jackie's face, brighter than any sun. As they stood there, hands entwined and hearts pounding, the workshop seemed to fade away, leaving only the two of them and the promise of a new beginning.

THE WARM GLOW of the setting sun poured in through the workshop windows, bathing Jackie and Marissa in a golden light as they stood side by side. The scent of sawdust lingered in the air, mingling with the faint aroma of their combined sweat after another day of hard work.

"Marissa," Jackie began, her voice filled with conviction. "I know this is new and scary for you, but I promise we'll take it slow." She gently squeezed Marissa's hand, making sure to maintain eye contact. "We can explore our desires and boundaries together, one step at a time."

A hesitant smile tugged at the corner of Marissa's lips, her heart racing at the thought of what lay ahead. "I appreciate that, Jackie. But how do we even begin?"

“Let’s go to a BDSM workshop?" Jackie asked, her eyes sparkling with excitement. "It's a place where people like us can gain a better understanding of what we enjoy."

"Really? That sounds... a good idea,” Marissa said, curiosity piqued. Her pulse quickened as she imagined herself surrounded by others who shared their desire for power exchange and pleasure.

"Trust me," Jackie assured her, her grip on Marissa's hand both comforting and enticing. "You'll be amazed at how much you can discover about yourself and your desires."

As the sun dipped below the horizon, casting long

shadows across the workshop floor, Marissa felt a surge of anticipation rise within her. The uncertainty that had plagued her thoughts seemed to dissipate, replaced by a sense of exhilaration she couldn't quite put her finger on.

"Alright, let's do it," Marissa agreed, her voice tinged with excitement. "Let's go to a workshop together."

"Perfect," Jackie beamed, a swell of pride filling her chest. "I know just the place."

The following weekend found them standing outside a nondescript building in the heart of the city, their breaths hitching as they took in the sounds of muffled moans and the faint scent of leather wafting from inside. Jackie squeezed Marissa's hand reassuringly, her confidence bolstering Marissa's resolve.

"Remember," Jackie whispered into Marissa's ear, sending shivers down her spine, "we're here to learn and explore. If anything feels too intense or uncomfortable, just let me know, and we'll stop immediately."

Marissa nodded, swallowing hard as her arousal began to stir at the thought of what lay behind those doors. Together, hand in hand, they stepped into a world of uncharted desires, ready to embrace the unknown and forge their own path.

CHAPTER FIVE

The dimly lit workshop buzzed with an electric energy, the air thick with anticipation. Jackie and Marissa stood among the eager participants, their fingers intertwined as they surveyed the array of activities laid out before them.

"Let's start with something simple," Jackie suggested, guiding Marissa towards a table laden with intricate rope designs. "Bondage can be a great way to build trust and explore vulnerability."

Marissa hesitated for a moment, her heart pounding in her chest as she imagined herself bound and at the mercy of another. She glanced at Jackie, whose unwavering gaze held nothing but encouragement and desire.

"Alright," Marissa breathed, allowing Jackie to lead her deeper into the world of restraint.

As Jackie expertly looped the soft rope around Marissa's wrists, binding them together with gentle precision, Marissa couldn't help but feel a surge of arousal course through her. The sensation of being restrained, albeit gently, was intoxicating.

"Is this too tight?" Jackie asked, concern lacing her words.

"No, it feels... good," Marissa admitted, her cheeks flushing with a mixture of embarrassment and excitement.

"Great," Jackie grinned, her eyes sparkling with mischief. "Now let's see how you like sensory play."

Jackie led Marissa to a station adorned with feathers, silk scarves, and other tactile items designed to titillate and tease. Gently blindfolding Marissa, Jackie began to trace the contours of her body with a soft feather, eliciting shudders of pleasure from her willing captive.

"Tell me what you're feeling, Marissa," Jackie murmured, her voice barely above a whisper.

"Desire," Marissa panted, her chest heaving as sensations rippled through her. "I want more."

"Good," Jackie whispered, her own desire mounting

as she watched Marissa's body tremble under her touch. "I want to push you, but only as far as you're comfortable."

"Push me," Marissa urged, feeling a thrill of anticipation at the thought of surrendering herself completely to Jackie's whims.

As Jackie continued to explore Marissa's body with an array of textures and sensations, they communicated openly about their preferences and boundaries. Marissa reveled in the vulnerability that came with being so exposed, finding herself craving more intensity with each touch.

"Jackie, I want to try something more daring," Marissa confessed, her voice quivering with excitement.

"Anything for you," Jackie replied, her heart swelling with affection for the woman who had entrusted her with such power. Together, they ventured into the realm of impact play, experimenting with floggers and paddles that left Marissa's skin flushed and sensitive.

Through every activity they engaged in, Jackie and Marissa maintained a level of honest communication that only served to deepen their connection. As they tested their limits and explored their desires, it became clear that this journey was not simply about physical pleasure; it was about forging an unbreakable bond built on trust, vulnerability, and love.

THE WORKSHOP'S cozy atmosphere was filled with the scent of leather and the soft murmur of voices as Jackie led Marissa through the gathering. Candlelight flickered across the attendees' faces, casting a warm glow on their flushed skin.

"Marissa, I'd like you to meet some people who have been really supportive in my exploration of BDSM," Jackie said, gently guiding her towards a small group engaged in quiet conversation.

"Hi, I'm Tessa," a woman with fiery-red hair and a wicked grin greeted them. "You must be Marissa. Jackie's told us so much about you."

"Nice to meet you," Marissa replied, trying to quell her nerves as she studied the others in the group. A tall woman with an air of authority stood beside Tessa, her arm draped possessively around her waist, while a petite woman wearing a collar and leash knelt at his feet.

"Marissa, this is Jane and her submissive, Lily," Jackie continued, making introductions.

"Welcome to our community," Jane said warmly, her

eyes holding a depth of wisdom that intrigued Marissa. Lily remained silent, but her shy smile spoke volumes about her trust in those around her.

"Thank you for having us," Marissa responded, aware of the comforting presence of Jackie at her side. She could sense the camaraderie among these individuals, all united by their mutual passion for BDSM.

"Jackie mentioned that you two are just starting to explore your roles," Tessa remarked, her gaze appraising. "It's important to experience both sides of the power dynamic to find what works best for you."

"Actually, we were hoping to give that a try tonight," Jackie chimed in, her green eyes alight with excitement.

"Excellent idea," Jane agreed. "It'll give you both a chance to discover your preferences and adapt to each other's needs."

"Shall we start with you, Marissa?" Tessa suggested, gesturing to a nearby padded bench. "You can take the dominant role first."

Marissa hesitated for a moment, her heart pounding as she considered the idea. She glanced at Jackie, seeking reassurance, and found it in the encouraging smile that graced her lips.

"Alright," Marissa agreed, determination settling in her chest. "I'll give it my best shot."

As she led Jackie towards the bench, Marissa felt an unfamiliar power surging within her. She instructed Jackie to bend over the padded surface, taking a deep breath to steady herself.

"Remember to communicate openly about your limits," Tessa reminded them, watching closely as the scene unfolded.

"Of course," Marissa replied, focusing on Jackie's exposed form before her. She trailed her fingertips down Jackie's spine, eliciting a shiver from her lover. The sensation of control was intoxicating, and Marissa reveled in every movement and reaction she could elicit from Jackie.

"Are you ready?" Marissa asked, her voice low and commanding.

"Please, Mistress," Jackie responded, using the honorific for the first time. A thrill coursed through Marissa at the sound, fueling her desire.

"Good girl," Marissa praised, experimenting with various implements and techniques while keeping a close eye on Jackie's reactions. She reveled in the trust placed in her hands, feeling their connection grow stronger with each strike.

Switching roles, Jackie took over as the dominant, guiding Marissa into a submissive position. As they explored this new dynamic, Marissa felt a sense of vulnerability that only heightened her arousal. Her body trembled under Jackie's firm touch and careful ministrations, the intensity of the experience unlike anything she had ever known.

"Thank you," Marissa whispered afterward, her eyes locked on Jackie's. "This was... incredible."

"Thank you for trusting me," Jackie replied, her voice filled with emotion. As they basked in the after-glow of their exploration, both women knew that they had stepped into uncharted territory – a world where trust, communication, and desire bound them together like never before.

THE DIM CANDLELIGHT flickered across the room, casting shadows that danced upon the walls. Marissa stood in the center, clad only in a delicate, black lace blindfold that concealed her deep blue eyes from Jackie's watchful gaze. The air was heavy with anticipation, and Marissa's heart raced as she awaited whatever surprise Jackie had planned for her.

"Marissa, I know we've been exploring our desires together," Jackie began, her voice husky and filled with emotion, "and I want to show you just how much your trust means to me."

As Marissa listened intently, she could hear the rustle of fabric as Jackie moved around the room. The scent of jasmine drifted through the air, its calming aroma mingling with the faint traces of leather and wax that pervaded their intimate space.

"Tonight, I've created a scene tailored to your fantasies... something I hope will bring us even closer," Jackie continued, her words sending a shiver down Marissa's spine.

"Jackie... I'm speechless," Marissa whispered, her voice trembling with gratitude and arousal. She couldn't believe the lengths to which Jackie was willing to go for her, and it stirred something within her – a desire to surrender completely and embrace the connection they shared.

"First, I want you to feel every touch, every sensation, without distraction," Jackie murmured, her fingers slowly trailing up Marissa's arm, causing goosebumps to rise on her skin. As she reached her shoulder, Jackie gently guided Marissa's arms behind her back, securing them with a soft silk rope. The pressure was firm, yet gentle, a testament to Jackie's skill and attention to detail.

"Next, I want you to experience the pleasure of anticipation," Jackie said as she circled Marissa, her footsteps barely audible against the plush carpet. The suspense built with each passing second, and Marissa's breathing grew heavier as she awaited Jackie's next move.

Suddenly, Marissa felt the lightest touch of a feather against her throat, making her gasp and arch her neck. The delicate caress continued, tracing patterns over her breasts, teasing her nipples until they stood erect and begging for attention. The sensation was maddening, igniting a fire deep within her core that demanded satisfaction.

"Jackie... please," Marissa whimpered, straining against her bonds in a futile attempt to touch herself. She could feel her desire pooling between her legs, the ache growing more insistent with each passing moment.

"Patience, my love," Jackie whispered, her breath warm against Marissa's earlobe. "Your pleasure is my priority tonight, but I want you to savor every moment."

As Jackie's words washed over her, Marissa felt something inside her begin to shift. Her doubts began to fade, replaced by a newfound trust in Jackie's devotion and an eagerness to explore the depths of their connection.

"Jackie... I'm ready," Marissa finally admitted, surrendering herself completely to the woman who had captured her heart and awakened her darkest desires.

"Then let us begin our journey together," Jackie murmured, pressing a tender kiss to Marissa's lips before guiding her down a path of exquisite pleasure that would forever change the course of their relationship.

CHAPTER SIX

Marissa lay next to Jackie, their chests rising and falling in perfect rhythm as they caught their breath from the intense scene they had just shared. The flickering candlelight danced across their skin, creating a sensual glow that highlighted the contrast between Jackie's lean, defined muscles and Marissa's soft, feminine curves. As she traced her fingers along Jackie's forearm, Marissa marveled at the newfound intimacy that seemed to envelop them like a protective cocoon, shielding them from the outside world.

"Jackie," Marissa whispered, her voice thick with emotion as she turned to face her lover. Her lips were still tingling from their passionate kisses and she couldn't believe how much more connected they felt in this moment. "I need to tell you something."

The sun set behind them, casting a golden glow on the two women. Jackie's emerald green eyes shone with affection and curiosity as she looked at Marissa. The air was filled with a sense of possibility, a feeling that anything could happen in this moment.

"Anything, my love," Jackie replied, her voice soft but full of sincerity.

Marissa's heart swelled with gratitude for the woman sitting across from her. "Being with you has opened up a whole new world for me," she confessed. "I've never felt this way before, not even with my husband. I didn't know it was possible to feel so deeply connected to someone, both emotionally and physically."

Jackie's hand reached out to tuck a strand of Marissa's golden hair behind her ear, a small gesture that sent shivers down her spine. "Neither did I, until I met you," she admitted. "You've changed my life, too."

Their gaze locked and time seemed to stand still as they looked into each other's eyes. Marissa knew it was time to be completely honest.

"I'm falling in love with you, Jackie," she said, her voice trembling with vulnerability and raw emotion. "And I'm willing to take whatever risks are necessary to be with you." In that moment, everything else faded away and all that mattered was the connection between them.

"Jackie's breath caught in her throat as tears glistened in her eyes. Marissa's hand squeezed hers, and Jackie knew that this was the moment. "I love you," she said, her voice trembling with emotion.

Marissa's blue eyes shone with determination as she suggested, "Let's make a promise to always support each other and explore our desires together, no matter what obstacles we may face."

With quivering lips, Jackie whispered her agreement and sealed their pact with a passionate kiss that conveyed all the love and commitment they shared.

With their hearts now fully aligned, Jackie and Marissa were ready to delve even deeper into the world of BDSM. As Marissa submitted to Jackie's loving dominance, she reveled in the sensation of being completely at her lover's mercy. Bound by silk rope, her body quivered with anticipation as Jackie's skilled hands worked their magic, teasing and tormenting her most sensitive areas with a mixture of pleasure and pain.

"Please, Jackie," Marissa moaned, her back arching as she felt the sharp sting of a riding crop on her inner thighs. "I need more."

Jackie's fingers trailed down Marissa's quivering

stomach, her touch igniting a fire that spread through every nerve in her body. Her lips brushed against Marissa's neck, sending shivers down her spine. "Be patient, my love," she whispered, her eyes filled with desire as she continued to tease and tantalize Marissa's throbbing flesh.

As Jackie slowly explored every inch of Marissa's body, pushing their boundaries and discovering new levels of pleasure together, Marissa knew that she had found her perfect match. Every touch, every kiss, every shared fantasy brought them closer together, their love growing stronger with each passing moment. And as they lay spent in each other's arms, their bodies intertwined like a living tapestry of passion and devotion, Marissa knew that their future held endless possibilities for adventure and fulfillment – all because of the love they shared with each other.

THE WARM GLOW of the flickering candlelight danced across the entwined bodies of Jackie and Marissa, casting shadows on their bare skin as they lay intertwined in the soft, satin sheets. The musky smell of sweat and desire hung heavy in the air, mixed with the sweet scent of vanilla from the candles. Their breathing gradually slowed, hearts beating in unison after the intense passion they had just shared.

"Jackie," Marissa breathed, her blue eyes shining with love and contentment as she gazed into her lover's emerald ones, "that was...indescribable.""Jackie," Marissa whispered, her blue eyes shining with emotion as she looked into her lover's green ones, "that was...incredible."

Jackie's bright smile warmed Marissa's heart, as she gently brushed a strand of damp hair from her forehead. "I'm so glad you enjoyed our time together, Marissa. I wanted to show you the incredible beauty and strength that can come from this kind of connection."

Every touch, every sensation...it was like discovering a part of myself I never knew existed. Marissa's soft, gentle hands traced patterns on Jackie's skin, awakening a fire within her that she couldn't deny. Her body responded eagerly to Marissa's touch, craving more and more of this newfound pleasure.

As they lay together in the afterglow, Jackie's heart swelled with pride and love for the woman who had come to mean everything to her. She took Marissa's hand in hers, fingers interlocking in a symbol of their bond.

"Marissa," Jackie spoke softly, her voice filled with sincerity and adoration. "Let's make a pact. We'll continue exploring our desires and boundaries together, taking this journey of discovery as far as it can go. We'll communicate openly and honestly about our feelings, our likes and dislikes, and support each other every step of the way. No matter what happens, we'll always be there for one another." With each word, Jackie felt a sense of excitement and trust building between them, solidifying their love and commitment to each other.

Marissa's eyes glistened with tears as Jackie poured her heart out, expressing their shared desire for a partnership built on trust, love, and their mutual passion for exploring this new world together. Marissa nodded eagerly, feeling a surge of warmth and affection in her chest.

"It's a promise," Jackie declared, locking her gaze with Marissa's. She leaned in slowly, their lips meeting in a tender yet intense kiss that seemed to last forever. As they parted, Jackie's hand trailed down Marissa's arm, sending shivers of pleasure through her body.

"I can't wait to see where this journey takes us, my love," Jackie whispered, caressing Marissa's cheek gently. The air around them felt charged with anticipation and excitement for the unknown future ahead.

Marissa traced small circles on Jackie's bare arm, feeling her skin tingle under her touch. With a soft sigh, she whispered, "I can't believe we finally did it." Her heart swelled with happiness and love as she snuggled closer to her partner, seeking the familiar warmth of their embrace.

As they lay there, surrounded by tangled sheets and breathless laughter, Marissa's mind raced with endless possibilities. Together, they would embark on a journey of passion and devotion, unafraid to explore the depths of their desires and hearts. And in that moment, they knew that no matter what challenges they may face, they would always have each other – bound not just by physical intimacy, but by an unbreakable bond of love.

Jackie gazed at Marissa, her chest rising and falling in a slow, steady rhythm. In the dimly lit room, the soft glow of candlelight played across the planes of her face, casting shadows and highlights that only added to her ethereal beauty. As her hand gently traced the outline of Marissa's jaw, Jackie's mind drifted to the future that lay before them.

The tender touches they had shared throughout the night had kindled a fire within her. It was a fire that could only be fueled by their mutual exploration of the BDSM lifestyle – a journey they were about to embark on together.

"Marissa," she whispered, her voice barely audible in the quiet room. "Are you ready for this journey?" The question hung in the air between them, charged with anticipation and desire. Jackie's heart raced as she waited for Marissa's answer, knowing that whatever it may be, it would lead them down an uncharted path filled with excitement and passion.

Marissa turned to face Jackie, her bright blue eyes shimmering with a mix of curiosity and desire. The sunlight danced off the flecks of gold in her irises, making them glitter like precious gems. "More than anything, Jackie," she said softly, "I trust you completely, and I can't wait to learn and grow alongside you."

Jackie's heart swelled with love and adoration as she gazed at Marissa. Her lips curved into a gentle smile as she reached out to tenderly brush a stray curl from Marissa's forehead, reveling in the softness of her skin. "I promise to always listen to your needs and desires," she murmured, "to push you but never overstep your boundaries."

Tears of happiness filled Marissa's eyes as she looked up at Jackie, overwhelmed with emotion.

"Thank you, my love," she whispered, "I promise the same to you. And I want you to know... I love you." As the words left her lips, a weight lifted from her heart and she felt a sense of peace wash over her, knowing that their love was strong and unbreakable.

Jackie's heart skipped a beat at the confession, her own love for Marissa swelling within her chest. "I love you too, Marissa. We'll face whatever challenges come our way, together."

With their promises exchanged, Jackie drew Marissa in for a gentle, passionate kiss, their tongues dancing together in a sensual choreography of love and devotion. As they broke apart, Jackie couldn't help but marvel at the beauty of the woman before her, the soft curves of her body illuminated by the pale moonlight filtering through the window.

"Let's get some rest, my love," Marissa suggested, her voice drowsy from their earlier activities. "We have a whole new world to explore, after all."

"Good idea," Jackie agreed, feeling the weight of her own exhaustion begin to settle in. She pressed a tender kiss to Marissa's temple before nestling into the crook of her arm, their bodies fitting together like two pieces of a puzzle.

As they drifted off to sleep, entwined in each other's arms, Jackie couldn't help but feel a sense of hope and anticipation for the future. The satin sheets draped over their bodies, caressing them with every move they made. Their breathing was synchronized, as if they were two parts of the same whole. Together, they would embark on a new chapter of their relationship, filled with love, trust, and the exploration of their shared desires.

Each adventure into the world of BDSM would bring them closer together, igniting sparks of passion and unlocking hidden layers of intimacy. And as they delved deeper into this alluring world, they would strengthen their bond in ways that neither could have ever imagined.

Milton Keynes UK
Ingram Content Group UK Ltd.
UKHW011831260224
438492UK00001B/48